THE MYSTERIOUS ANIMAL SOUP

AND
RACHEL'S GIFTS

RONY KESSLER

Dedicated to my children and grandchildren.

CONTENTS

INTRODUCTION

Rachel, a young girl, survives a horrible crime and loses her voice, but not her determination to solve the tragedy that has befallen her family. **Rony Kessler's** novel that occurs in both the US and the Middle East, is a riveting page turner, that pits Rachel a Twelve-year-old, against a gang of thugs that attacked her family. **"The Mysterious Animal Soup, and Rachel's Gifts"** follows the short prequel **"The Professor and the Wild Dogs"**

ACKNOWLEGEMENTS

Thanks to my wife, Ana, for all her help and
encouragement.
I truly appreciate the great suggestions and advice from my
Tween Editors:
Lilah, Dahlia and Gabriel Cohen,
Isabella Diaz, Avery Diaz, and Selah Kessler.
Thanks to my daughter, Robin, and my friends Eric and
Valerie Shoenfeld, Bill Youngfert, and Rabbi Art Vernon, my
first readers.
Thanks also to:
Stephanie from Red Penguin Books for her direction and
advice.

PROLOGUE

Humans have been the most successful species in history. We have multiplied in numbers and have dominated all forms of life, except maybe for the mosquitoes and the virus. Viruses, however, are not really living things. To survive and make more of themselves, they need a host, like your body or that of an animal. While the evolution (slow, gradual changes) of humans has certainly made us smarter, our senses have actually become less sharp. We invented vehicles to make us faster, created hearing aids and listening devices to make us hear better, and invented eyeglasses and binoculars for us to see better and farther. But we have not been able to improve the performance of our senses in a natural way.

We have had success in improving animal abilities. The liger is a combination of a tiger and a lion. Mating a horse and a donkey in captivity created the mule. It was designed to be strong and to work in the fields. As successful as these matings were, the liger and mule could not have babies.

Many successful changes were made by combining animals with certain abilities or traits. The oldest that comes to mind is the domestication of the wolf, making the wolf tame, so that he can live with us without eating us. This was done by mating a calm male wolf, with a calm female wolf so that calm puppies were born. By continuing this process over and over, the wolf became tame, house broken, and our best friend, the dog.

We have many varieties of dogs today that came about through selective mating over many generations. Dogs have been bred for specific roles, such as bull dogs, sheep dogs, guard dogs, dogs catering to the blind and drug enforcement agencies, and bomb-sniffing dogs. We even have dogs today that can sniff out oncoming health issues for diabetics and sniff and point out a person with a virus or cancer. Of course, we cannot forget show dogs that are bred for their beauty or special look. Most of these results were achieved by breeding a dog with a particular natural ability to another of the same ability in order to make that ability better, thereby improving the sense of smell, for example. The same would be true to make the dog's speed, strength, or intelligence better. In farming, cows were bred to give more milk. Rodeo bulls were bred to jump wildly and buck better so that it would be a challenge for the rider and more entertaining for the crowd. Horses were bred for speed, endurance, strength, jumping, and even for entertaining, like the famous Lipizzaner stallions. They were originally trained for the military. Then, these beautiful white horses became performing wonders, trained to perform feats that amaze and entertain.

The manipulation of changing, adding, or taking away genes has spread to fish, chickens, ducks, and even plants.

Many in the science community became worried about the long-term effects for the future. They were concerned about the effects of eating and digesting manipulated food. They were worried that the DNA changes might show up in potential mutations, which means changes in the DNA of humans. The scientists were worried that many human creations might affect people later in life or perhaps their children. Many wonderful drugs that helped a lot of people after being in use for a long time resulted in unexpected bad results and had to be stopped from being sold.

It has been accepted by the world's scientific community that certain experiments in breeding and genetic manipulations are not wise or ethical. The determination of what is and is not acceptable or moral has been taken over by medical panels and state and federal laws in many countries. Many countries allow parents and their doctors to decide if a baby should be a boy or a girl. It is also accepted in many countries that parents and their doctors can make sure that a baby will not have certain diseases (genetic diseases).

Experiments advanced constantly, and the world was shocked when the famous sheep, Dolly, was created in a laboratory in England that was identical to another sheep that was born naturally. The process is called cloning, making an exact duplicate. That knowledge eventually led to human cloning by a scientist in China. It scared a lot of people and was met with disapproval. The fear of unwanted mutations (changes) in humans that could have unintended and bad consequences led to it being prohibited.

The animal world is amazing. It is well known that many mammals, fowl, even insects possess abilities that are far greater than ours. While there is no question that we are the smartest, we are not the champs when it comes to hearing, vision, smell, taste, or touch. Bears have an amazing sense of smell. It has been reported that black bears have been observed to travel as many as 18 miles in a straight line to a food source. Grizzlies can find an elk carcass when it's underwater, and polar bears can smell a seal through three feet of ice. Elephants are known, not only for how big their ears are but also how well those ears function. Elephants have an uncanny sense of smell for water and an amazing memory for where the water sources are, year after year.

Eagles can see eight times as far as humans. They can locate a small animal from a mile up in the sky. Owls have excellent night vision, as well as hearing. We all know about homing pigeons finding their way home after being released hundreds of miles away. How about salmon? They are able to find the stream where they hatched after roaming the oceans, have the ability to leap many times their size out of the water, and to climb over obstacles. Insects can be champs, as well. Moths have been nominated as having the best hearing, ants have enormous strength for their size, and I am sure there are hundreds, if not thousands, of other examples.

CHAPTER 1

THE ATTACK

S he woke up with a start. She heard something, and it did not sound right. They were very quiet, but she heard them. She was only twelve years old, too inexperienced to know that she was not supposed to be capable of hearing that well. It was not normal; people did not normally have the kind of hearing she did. No one else could probably hear the noise that awoke her, but she did not know that. She was never an ordinary child, having perfect recall and sharp senses that defied the normal spectrum. She was wise for her years and talented beyond convention. Adults who met her were always amazed at her maturity and her quickness. Friends of their parents would say, "She can't be six" or "she can't be seven."

Now, when her mom would give her age as twelve, they would say, "Wow, she is so smart." Her mom would smile proudly and say, "Rachel is my twelve-year-old going on twenty."

Somehow, even though they eased into the house like

ghosts, she could hear them clearly. First, the screen door sliding open, and then the glass door. There were several separate footsteps, rubber soles on the tiled floors, she counted five of them. They moved fast. They were now on the steps. She could hear the imperceptible creaking of the steps under their weight as they slowly crept up the stairs. Who were they and what did they want?

Rachel thought that it might be a dream; maybe this was not real. She really was not sure. She lay awake listening with her heart thumping, practically jumping out of her chest. Her throat was constricting so she could hardly swallow. Her brother John, they called him Johnny, in whose bed she was, lay sleeping soundly next to her. Johnny was on his side facing away from her, breathing deeply. Rachel slowly uncovered herself and got out of the bed. She wanted to go to her father's room to warn him, but the men were already in the hallway. Johnny was only six and the youngest of her three siblings. She was his big sister, the eldest of four. She was the one he always went to for security. Last night he insisted that she sleep with him in his bed and her mom agreed to let her. She was always happy to accommodate him since he had a big bed, much bigger than hers. She thought that it was clever of her because her bed would not get messed up, and she would not have to make it up in the morning. She had no idea how this little fact would impact her young life tonight.

Rachel moved slowly towards the door of the room, one of several on the second floor, which had five bedrooms and her dad's office. It was a long corridor with three rooms on either side. At the top of the stairs to the left was her parents' bedroom.

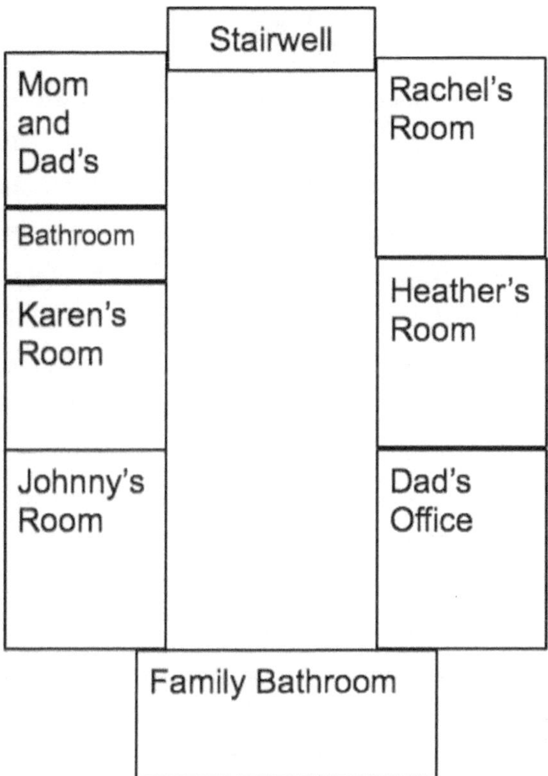

Across from her parents' bedroom was her room. On the left after her parents' room was Karen's room, her ten-year-old sister. Across from her was Heather's room, her eight-year-old sister. Johnny's room, in which she was now in, was on the left at the end of the hall across from her father's office. At the end of the hall was the family bathroom the kids used since her parents had their own bathroom in their bedroom.

She got to Johnny's bedroom door just as the first of the men was in the hallway and next to her father's door. She could not get to him now. She peeked out the door and could see the one man in the hall gesturing to the others. Rachel should not have been able to see them at all because it was very dark in the house at nighttime. The men were all in the hall now outside her parents' door. She could hear them breathing. They were wearing black outfits and funny glasses, big fat glasses. Rachel saw these glasses in a movie once. She remembered the movie, *Mission Impossible*. She remembered that her dad said that they could make people see in the dark. Rachel had asked her father why they needed them. She thought that everyone could see like her. Her father explained that these glasses, called night goggles, used the tiniest traces of light to amplify them so that they could see when there was no visible light. He explained that it was mainly used by the military and the police. Rachel was still puzzled, but for some reason did not question him further or wonder why anyone would need them. She could see in the dark without them. She did not realize that she was not supposed to see in the dark. She thought everyone did.

As she stood at the door, she wondered if the men were military or police. The men were gesturing to each other, or more accurately, she realized that it was the first one up that was gesturing to everyone else. Somehow, she knew by intuition that he was the leader. Rachel could see him clearly. He looked athletic and had a scar on his throat. He gestured to himself and pointed to her parents' bedroom door and then to each door down the hall. First, he pointed to one man and then to her door, then to the next man and to Heather's door, then to Karen's door, and finally to Johnny's door where she was standing. Five men, five bedrooms. She was not in her room, nor did she sleep there tonight; but one of the men was heading there, and one of them was heading towards her, right where she was standing peering out. She did not know what to do. Should she scream? Should she try to run to Karen's room to alert her? Should she hide? The man who gestured to the others had his hand on her parents' door handle; and the others, the four men with him, started moving towards the other rooms and towards her. She saw the leader of the group open her parents' door. He entered the room. She saw that he and the others had guns in their hands with long barrels. That was when she decided to scream.

Rachel opened her mouth and expected to hear herself scream, but nothing came out. It was as though her throat was paralyzed. She tried again, but nothing came out, no sound! She thought of bolting across the hall, but the men were in the hall coming towards Johnny's room. As she turned to look for a place to hide in her brother's room, she heard a spitting sound like soft whispers, pfft... pfft... pfft... She quickly backed up into the room out of sight. She turned and ran towards her brother's bed. He was still sleeping soundly. She was going to get into the bed and cover them both and hide under the blanket. Then she thought she would get under the bed. It was then that she saw the chest where her mother stored the blankets at night. Johnny's spare blanket was still in there. Without thinking, survival instinct took over, and she dove into the chest which was at the foot of the bed and somehow was able to squeeze in and get the fluffy blanket on top of her so that it covered her completely.

It was stuffy and tough to breathe, but it was also timely. It was not with a moment to spare as one of the men came into the room. The man came closer to the bed. She could hear his footsteps and his breathing. A few seconds later she heard another man from the hallway talking to the man inside the room in a whispered voice, a voice with a very thick accent, "Yaya, I went to the girl's room and she was not in there. I checked the room, the bed was not slept in."

The man by the bed, who was called Yaya, whispered back, also with a very thick accent, "It's obvious if her bed was not slept in, then the girl is either in one of the other rooms or maybe slept out at a friend or relative."

The man, who she now figured was standing by the door in the hall, said, "Salim will not be happy."

The man who was addressed as Yaya said, "Stop talking stupid, Ishy, before we wake the boy up! Let's do what we came here to do and get out. We will worry about the girl later."

Rachel's nostrils flared as she smelled a strange odor. It was medicinal, one she had not smelled before. She heard a sound like someone ruffling the bedding and then lifting something up. Then she heard Karen scream. It was not a normal scream. It was the kind of scream that was being blocked by a hand over someone's mouth. She knew that because sometimes when they played, they did that to each other. It was a game they played, how loud can you scream with a hand over your mouth. It was probably why Karen was able to make such a loud sound; she had done that before. The voice from the door that she now knew was called Ishy said, "I wonder what is happening over there? They were supposed to use the ether to put her to sleep."

"Raja can never do anything quietly," the man called Yaya said. "Saud should be watching him." She heard sounds of lifting, and then she heard the one called Yaya leave the room saying, "Ishy, let's go check on Raja." She could hear them walk down the hall, and she could tell they went to Karen's room. She lifted the blanket, got out of the cubby, and went over to Johnny's bed. Johnny was not there. She realized with horror that this man Yaya took her Johnny.

Rachel's body went rigid. She was not only scared, she was confused, and she was mad. WHY? Why would they take Johnny? What did he do to them? Who are they? Was she still dreaming?   That's it, this must be a dream, she thought. Finally, she decided she would check on her mom and dad, and they would make it okay. She went to the door slowly and peeked across the hall. She was not sure if it was safe. She could hear one man say, "Let's go and carry them out." It sounded like the man Salim giving orders. He said, "Yaya, Ishy, come back when you are done and go to the office and get everything." He and two of the men were walking down the hall carrying big black bags, so she moved back into the room. After she heard the men all leave, she wanted to sneak down the hall into her father's room; but she heard footsteps coming up the steps to the hall again. She guessed the two men came back to go to the office to get something as Salim ordered. She peeked out again and saw them carrying big boxes down the stairs. She later surmised that this was what they were after, but why did they take Johnny? What were they doing? What was in the big black bags?

As the two called Yaya and Ishy walked down the steps carrying two boxes each, Yaya said to Ishy, "I hate taking kids, that Salim has no conscience."

Ishy replied, "He has a lot of history with the family so it's really sad."

Rachel waited a few minutes after they went down and then she walked down the hall quietly to go check on her parents and see what the men did. She slowly took one step after the other, snuck down the hallway, and crept into her parents' bedroom. All the lights were still out in the house; the only light in the room was from the little red numbers on the VCR and their radio alarm clock. The clock said 3:30. The VCR was flashing 12:00. It was a joke between her mom and her dad because they never figured out how to make that VCR clock work. Her mother was lying in bed facing her father's side of the bed, but her father was not next to her. Where was her dad? Still moving slowly one step at a time, her bare foot suddenly stepped on a piece of metal or something. She cried out OUCH, but no sound came out. Her throat still felt frozen. She put her hand down on the floor and picked up what looked like a small metal cylinder. It had a sharp edge on the end. She put it in her pajama pocket. She moved closer to the bed; and when she reached it, she grabbed her mother's foot. It was very cold and she shook it...nothing happened. Her mom did not react. Rachel tickled the foot, something that always got a giggle out of her mom, still nothing. She tried to say mom, but nothing came out of her mouth.

I must be dreaming, Rachel thought, because in real life I can talk. Her intuition told her, though, that this was not a dream and the fact that her mom was not responding was awfully bad. She looked for her father and finally found him. He was on the floor on his side of the bed. She went to him and he seemed to be sleeping. She nudged him, but he did not respond. Then she saw a trickle of blood coming out of his ear. She ran down to Karen's room, but she was not in her bed. She looked everywhere thinking maybe she was hiding, too; but she did not find her. She noticed that smell again, was that ether that Yaya mentioned? She ran to Heather's room, but she was not there either. She was all alone with her mother and father who were dead.

Rachel returned to her parents' bedroom looking for the phone. She had to call for help. Where did they take Johnny, Karen, and Heather? Why did they shoot her mother and father? What was in the boxes? She did not understand. She wanted to know why she could not scream. She questioned herself, why didn't she confront the men or do something? She knew she had to call the police, maybe they could catch the men and get Karen, Heather, and Johnny back.

She blinked away tears as she looked at her mother and father lying immobile. Her mother was on the bed and her father next to the bed. Rachel realized that her world had become very, very different. It was not a visual difference and it was not her sight that told her the difference, it was some other part of her brain that processed it. It was not memory or intelligence. It was like an instinct, subconscious knowledge, just like knowing it was daylight or nighttime. She ran out of her parents' room. Her heart was beating so fast she thought she would pass out again. She went downstairs carefully, though she figured no one was there since there was only silence.

As she went down the steps, her muscles were so tight they hurt. Her teeth were clenched so tightly that she thought she would never be able to unclench them. She saw nothing out of the ordinary in the rooms on the first floor. The house was still dark, but she had no trouble finding the phone in the kitchen. The phone, an old one that came with the house, was a wall phone with a rotary dial. She picked up the phone from its holder and dialed 911. She heard the phone ring twice, and then she heard a voice say, "Cincinnati police, emergency, State your emergency please!" Her mouth started moving as it normally would when she started talking.

She wanted to yell out "MY MOM AND MY DAD ARE DEAD AND MY BROTHER AND SISTERS WERE KIDNAPPED!" but nothing came out. She heard the voice say "Hello, hello. Is someone there?" In frustration, Rachel started banging the phone against the wall. BANG! BANG!

BANG! She heard the operator say again louder, "HELLO, HELLO, IS SOMEONE THERE?" She banged the phone again, this time more calmly, not in frustration, like she just did a second ago. She banged in a rhythm, BANG! BANG! BANG! Pause, BANG! BANG! BANG! Pause, BANG! BANG! BANG! Then she heard the operator say to someone else, "Hey Rose, this is really weird. I just got a call, someone is there, but all I hear is banging"

Her sharp hearing could actually pick up the other woman's voice whose name was Rose, say, "Well, get the number. I will get the address and send a unit to the house!" Gosh, she is a smart person, this Rose, Rachel thought.

Then she heard the operator that answered her call say to the woman that she now knew as Rose, "I don't know, you really think I should?" When she heard him say that, she started banging the phone again in the same rhythmic cadence as before. BANG! BANG! BANG! Pause, BANG! BANG! BANG! Pause, BANG! BANG! BANG!

She kept that up for a while, and when she listened again, the voice of the original operator said "Okay, okay, we are sending a unit. If you understand what I just said, bang the phone twice." She did. BANG! BANG!

Within a few minutes she heard sirens, wheels screeching, and then a car pulling up outside. She ran to the door, undid the chain, disengaged the lock, and then pulled hard on the heavy door. As she did all that, Rachel's brain processed almost without her thinking about it consciously, that the men who killed her parents obviously did not go out through the front door, since it was locked from the inside. When the door was finally open, she realized with surprise that it might have taken her a while to open the door. The policeman was already standing in front of the open screen door, which he obviously had opened.

The screen door was held open with his left hand and he had his right hand on his gun. "Hi, little girl", he said. "Is your daddy or mommy home?" he asked. She looked at him like he was the biggest dope she had ever seen. Why would he have had to be summoned here with knocks of the phone against the wall if her mommy and daddy were here? She gestured for him to come in and pointed up the stairs. He took a tentative step in and looked right then left, like he anticipated an ambush or something. She tugged at his shirt sleeve to hurry him along and he said, "Okay," very loudly at first, and then, "okay" in a softer voice, "let me just call in." He picked up his walkie-talkie or whatever it was from his belt buckle and said into it, "Hey, Sarge, this is Mike. I am at 330 Greenfield Avenue. There is just a young girl here and she wants me to go upstairs. She evidently is mute. What do you want me to do? OVER!"

Boy, Rachel thought, they must have picked the dumbest guy to send here. The phone crackled and the voice of Sarge came back, "Well, go upstairs. WHAT ARE YOU WAITING FOR? And let me know what is happening, OVER!"

"ROGER and OUT!" said her genius officer Mike, who now started walking towards the stairs. "Is this where you want me to go?" he said. She just ignored him and continued to walk towards the steps. "I guess you can't hear, either," he said. She did not even bother to turn around. She just started to go up the stairs with the policeman behind her. When she got to the top of the stairs, she pointed to her parents' room but did not go in. Mike the Policeman looked at her and shouted, "IN THERE?" Rachel had no idea why he was shouting. She guessed that he decided that if she couldn't talk, she couldn't hear either, but then why would he shout? Did he think that she somehow might hear his screaming even though she couldn't hear? She nodded her head and pointed her finger in the direction of the room.

"HOLY MOTHER OF CHRIST!" she heard him shout. Tears started rolling down her eyes. Somehow, she was too keyed up and had not acknowledged any of it consciously, like it did not really happen. But now it was real. She felt her throat tighten up again and her chest hurt. Mike came out with a look of horror. She pointed to the other rooms. He went first to her room, and saw that the bed was not slept in. Mike then went to Heather's room and to Karen's room. Both beds were slept in, but the children were not there. Finally he went into Johnny's room. When he came out he said, "Young lady, where are the other children?" She made a gesture like someone carrying a sack on their shoulder and motioned downstairs.

Mike went back into her parents' room and once inside, he was on the walkie-talkie again calling his sergeant. "Hey Sarge, I got two murders here. I checked their pulses. They are both deceased. Looks like someone killed this guy and his wife and maybe kidnapped the children." He continued, "One young girl survived. She is with me. You better send some help over!"

Rachel heard a voice coming from the instrument, must be the sergeant, she thought. "Don't touch anything and watch what you say in front of the girl, OVER!" came the voice.

"Don't worry about the little girl. She is mute, and I think she can't hear, either. She is outside the bedroom. She can't hear me, OVER!" Rachel thought it was really something. This guy thinks I can't hear. She could hear him breathe.

She heard the sergeant's voice again, "Get the girl out of there and DON'T TOUCH ANYTHING! OVER!"

Mike replied, "OKAY, ROGER and OUT!" Mike the Policeman came out and she pointed to the other rooms and shook her head emphatically. She wanted him to look for her brother and sisters.

All of a sudden, it hit her like a bolt of lightning. She was all alone. Her throat felt frozen again. It was like the time she ate ice cream too fast. It was not only her throat, but her whole brain was freezing. As the shock of it all started to fade away a little, it dawned on her that she was all alone. Her mom and dad were dead; and Johnny, Heather, and Karen were gone. She started shaking like she had a fever or something. Then she felt Mike the Policeman put his arm around her and say, "Come with me downstairs. Don't be afraid. My name is Mike and I will look after you. Don't you worry, you're in good hands." His voice was calmer, more father-like, as he said, "I have a daughter just like you at home and my heart is breaking for you." As he walked downstairs with her, she realized that he was talking to her the way she used to talk to her dolls sometimes. She knew they could not understand and could not answer, but she talked to them anyway. "I don't know how anyone can do that to a family" Mike continued "He must have done something really bad to someone." Rachel thought he was trying to be nice, but he was not doing anything. She hoped that as soon as the others arrived, they would see what these bad guys did and go get them.

Mike the Policeman walked outside the door with her. It was just getting light outside, the light before sunrise. The day was just beginning. Rachel thought that it was all wrong, it should be bleary and rainy and cold. It should not be a nice day. She could hear the sirens long before they were anywhere near the house. It was like a scene from the movies. First came a second police car, and Rachel was surprised when the driver got out and she saw that the driver was a police woman. Somehow, police women did not compute in her brain. The woman came over and said, "Mike, I will take the girl." She asked Mike if he knew her name.

"No," Mike said, "She's deaf and mute."

The police woman said, "She might just be in shock." Rachel thought, they are already getting smarter. The woman took her around her shoulder as Mike did. She smelled nice like her mother. "Hi, young lady. My name is Mary. What's yours?" She really wanted to tell her and actually thought she said Rachel, but nothing came out. The police woman, Mary, saw her mouth moving and figured that she was trying to tell her. She said, "Well, don't worry about it right now. We will figure things out."

The activity in the street and in her driveway increased steadily. Ambulances came, another truck with "CORONER" written on it pulled up. Lots of guys came and went. They all put these white booties on their shoes and wore gloves. They also put yellow tape all around the house and on both ends of her street. Then she noticed a black limo roll up to the yellow tape. What was a limo doing there, she wondered. Two men got out of the limo and leaned against the car. They were dressed in black with dark sunglasses. They just stood there and looked at the activity but did not talk to anyone or do anything. They just stood there. A big truck arrived, and policemen got out with more yellow tape and started stretching it around the trees in the front and the back, going all around the house. They began to literally crawl around the lawn and the sidewalk looking for clues. That was more like it, she thought. Now they will start looking for the killer kidnappers. Then they will find my Johnny, Karen, and Heather.

Mary the police woman ushered her to a police car, opened the back door, and motioned her to the seat. Then she called another policeman," Harry! Drive us to the station!" The policeman, Harry, got in the driver's seat and Mary got in next to Rachel. She got a blanket from somewhere and laid it on her. She was still in her pajamas, Rachel realized. She also had blood on her hands. She wondered how the blood got on her hands, then remembered that she touched her dad's head where he was shot, and she shivered. Mary wrapped the blanket tighter around her and put her arms around her. They drove for a while and then they pulled in front of a big building. She realized it was the police station. Why are they taking me here, she wondered?

Harry and Mary did not talk during the ride, but now Harry asked, "What is going to happen to her now?" Mary said that she had to contact Child Services and see if they can find relatives. Mary directed her up the stairs into the station. Rachel realized that she was in her house shoes.

Once in the station, it seems everyone knew who she was

by their comments. "Poor Kid," "How is she doing?" and so on.

Mary walked her up a flight of stairs to a room that had a table and some chairs and motioned her to a chair. "Are you hungry?" she asked, "or thirsty?" Rachel shook her head. Based on Rachel responding, Mary figured she could lip read, she just needed to make sure she faced her. "Can you write for me?" Mary asked. Rachel thought, I'm 12, of course I can write. She nodded her head yes. Mary pulled out a pad and some pencils from a drawer and placed them in front of her. I know you have been through a lot, and it must be terribly hard for you; but we need to get as much information as we can so hopefully we can find your siblings. Rachel nodded her head enthusiastically. Mary started by asking her what her name is, and Rachel wrote her name on the paper, *RACHEL GLICK*. She had a neat and beautiful handwriting. Mary complimented her penmanship and wondered at the same time why it surprised her. Somehow, because she could not hear, she assumed that all her senses and abilities were impaired. It was a conclusion that was the opposite from reality, since most of the time when a child or an adult loses one of the senses, their other senses become stronger and work better. Mary asked, "Do you have any relatives or someone that we can contact to come and be with you?"

Rachel wrote, "Aunt Ruthie. Her name is Ruth Mintz, my daddy's sister." Mary asked her if she knew where she lived, and Rachel wrote, "New York."

"Is there anyone else? Friends that your father and or mother are close to?" Rachel shook her head no.

Mary asked Rachel again if she wanted something to eat

or drink. She realized that it was probably normal breakfast time already. Rachel wrote, "I usually have orange juice and cereal." Mary told her she would be back in a few minutes and left the room. In the hall, she called a woman named Dawn and asked her to look up Ruth Mintz in New York. She then asked someone else to bring orange juice, cereal, and milk to Rachel and, of course, a spoon, sugar and napkins. When she came back, she told Rachel that they were working on finding Aunt Ruth and that the food was coming. Rachel wrote, "I use the orange juice in my cereal, so I don't need the milk you ordered."

Mary looked up surprised, she said, "How did you know I ordered milk?"

Rachel wrote, "I heard you!"

Mary looked confused and said, "I thought you couldn't hear?"

Rachel wrote, "I can hear fine, but something happened to my voice last night. When I tried to scream, nothing came out." Mary realized that there was a lot they did not know about last night.

A few minutes later a young policeman came in with the juice, the cereal, and the milk. Mary gave the milk back to him. When the young man looked at her, she shrugged her shoulders with a smile and told him that Rachel puts orange juice in her cereal. The young man said, "I never heard of people eating cereal with orange juice."

Mary said, "Well, you heard it now." A woman came into the room a while later, Rachel could not tell how much time passed. She had a tape recorder and a pad and sat down opposite her. Mary introduced them. "This is Dawn," she said. "She is a detective and wants to ask you some questions about last night."

Rachel was eating her cereal with the orange juice and looked at Dawn with curiosity. Dawn checked Rachel out. She looked mature beyond her age. She had super long, wavy brown hair and light brown eyes. She was tall for her age, it seemed, maybe five foot two or so. Dawn said "We are working on finding and contacting your Aunt Ruth Mintz. We hope we can find her soon." She turned on the tape recorder and said, "Can you tell me what you remember about last night?"

Mary interjected "She cannot speak, and I think it's shock induced."

Dawn asked Rachel, "Can you write?" Rachel nodded her head yes. She thought some of these people were like Mike the Policeman, dumb. I just wrote all over the pad, didn't she see? Dawn asked her, "So can you write for me what you remember about last night?" as she shut off the tape recorder. Rachel nodded her head yes and picked up the pen Dawn handed her.

Rachel wrote: *Five men came into our house, killed my mom and dad, and then took my brother and my two sisters and left. They also took two boxes. I called the police.*

Dawn looked puzzled and said, "I thought you cannot talk. How did you call the police?"

Mary interjected, "She is a very clever girl; she banged the phone in rhythm and let us know by the banging that she needed help."

Dawn nodded her head and said, "Wow, you are a clever young lady. I am so sorry about your loss. I hope we hear from your aunt soon. In the meantime, Child Services will be here later, just in case." Mary said that she would stay with Rachel and then Dawn left. Later, a nice young policeman brought them chicken fingers and French fries. Rachel was a little reluctant since her mom did not let them eat fast food; but eventually, her hunger made her get over the guilt and she dived into the food. After they ate, Rachel put her head down on the table and fell asleep. It was as much exhaustion after not sleeping since the attack as it was wanting to escape the memories of the night that kept flooding back.

It was several hours later that Dawn came back with the news that they located her aunt and she was on the way from New York to Cincinnati.

A tall older woman with a head full of white hair and big black-rimmed glasses came into the room. She introduced herself as Mrs. Bartov from Child Services. Mary told her briefly that they were waiting for Rachel's aunt who was on her way from New York. Mary suggested that they go outside so she could bring her up to date. When Mary and Mrs. Bartov came back, they both were moist eyed; and she asked Rachel when she last saw her aunt. Rachel wrote that the last time she had seen Aunt Ruthie, as they called her, was at her sister Heather's birthday party when she was eight, a few months ago. Rachel wrote that before that, she saw her on the Passover holiday, two years ago. Mrs. Bartov said to Mary as though they were ending a conversation, "Okay, we will wait for Rachel's aunt. In the meantime, I will make arrangements for them to stay at a hotel. I don't think they can go back to the house, nor will the police allow anyone to go into it anyway. It's a crime scene."

It was late in the evening when Aunt Ruthie rushed into

the room and hoisted Rachel out of the seat, hugging her tightly. It took Mary and Mrs. Bartov by surprise, but Mary was touched and, on some level, relieved when Rachel began to sob for the first time since she picked her up at the house. Aunt Ruthie was now crying, too; and Mary and Mrs. Bartov were not dry-eyed themselves.

Rachel felt the vibrations of the plane. It must be pretty windy out there, she thought. She wondered what it would be like to fly like a bird. She was sitting next to her Aunt Ruthie on a big jet heading to New York. She was still numb from all that had happened, numb, incredibly sad, and very, very angry. Her voice had still not returned, but she was able to communicate by hand signs and writing.

She remembered her time in the police station. With her unusually sharp hearing she could hear the officers talk. "Poor kid, she must be devastated. Can you imagine a young girl like her going through something like that?"

She heard a detective say, "These men must have done a good job when they left. I understand they left no clues." She heard them say that there were no footprints outside, the front door was latched, and Mike the Policeman said he heard her undo the chain, so it had to be someone they knew or very good operators. Rachel remembered undoing the chain, but she figured that they must have gone out the back. She heard the detectives, when they talked amongst themselves, say that the back door was locked, as well. How did they lock the door behind them, she thought.

Her Aunt Ruth and Uncle Joe, who had no children, had come and stayed with her in Cincinnati for the past six months. They were wonderful. First, they rented a suite in a hotel, and then they moved into a rented apartment. They would not let her go back to the house. Rachel begged them to let her go back there, but they thought it was best that she not go. They brought her clothes, games and schoolbooks from the house and tried to do the best they could for her. At first, some of the kids from her class visited with some of the teachers, but soon they stopped coming. She could not speak, and they were always uncomfortable. It was difficult to just hang out without conversation.

Only Robin, her teacher, kept coming every week. She brought her the class work and reviewed homework that she assigned. She always brought her something to play with or something to do that did not require her speaking. She had so much patience, and the best thing about her was that she treated her normally. She did not try to patronize her or treat her with pity, something everyone else did. Even her Aunt Ruth and Uncle Joe stepped gingerly around her, always watching what they said. Rachel found it kind of silly since she could hear everything they said anyway, even when they were alone in the kitchen or in their bedroom. Aunt Ruthie, a psychologist and a writer of children's books, saw every-thing as emotionally based. She worked out of the home even when she saw patients, which was rare since her prac-tice was in New York. She did not know many people in

Cincinnati, and she made friends with Mrs. Bartov who still came around to see her. Mrs. Bartov referred a few clients to her which kept her busy. Aunt Ruthie was very protective of her and made it a point to stay near her almost all the time. The only adult that Aunt Ruthie left her with was her teacher Robin when she came over to work with her. Since she was now considered handicapped, both physically and emotionally, she was homeschooled; and somehow Mrs. Bartov and Aunt Ruth got Robin to be assigned to work with her. She would hear Robin tell Aunt Ruthie, "Go out for a while. Get your nails done or something."

And her aunt would say, "Thanks, Robin. I think I will. You know, you are the only one who really perks Rachel up."

Rachel, while slowly adjusting to life without her mom, dad, Johnny, Heather, and Karen, still often replayed that horrible night in her head. She did not want to lose any of the facts she remembered, and she did not forget a minute. There was Yaya who she was sure took Johnny, Ishy who was supposed to take her because he came to tell Yaya she was not in her room. Then there was Saud who she thinks took Heather, and Raja who made Karen scream, then took her. She remembered the smell of what she knew now was ether. She remembered the men talking in her room mentioning, "Salim will be unhappy." She had concluded long ago that he was the leader. Salim, Yaya, and Ishy all had an accent. That accent, she could not forget that accent. She knew now that the accent was Arabic. She knew she would not forget it, and she planned to eventually find out exactly where the accent originated. She realized that it was from somewhere in the Middle East.

She also remembered those glasses that could see in the

dark, the night goggles, and the rubber shoes. Her mind stored the faces she saw, too. Though it was dark, she could see and she remembered everything. But what happened to her voice? Her aunt kept telling her it would come back, but it did not; and she did not understand how it could just disappear. Her Aunt Ruthie told her it was from the trauma, the shock; and she said that in her experience, that kind of problem could be corrected, but Rachel had to find a way to let that terrible night go. She really wanted to let it go, and she promised herself that when her voice came back the first thing she would do was let out a huge scream. She still felt responsible and guilty for not screaming or, at the minimum, for not protecting Johnny. She could have tried to hide him or lock the door or something, but she never expected these men to kidnap Johnny. What did he do to them? Why did they shoot her parents and take Johnny, Heather, and Karen?

If anything made her blind with rage, it was the fact that they had not allowed her to see her parents at the funeral, it was conducted with closed caskets. All the people at the funeral home, most of whom she did not know, came and said the same thing to her, but she was not paying attention. She was thinking about her brother and sisters; she wanted them found. People kept on talking about closure; but until she found them, she knew there would be no closure. The tradition in the Jewish religion was to sit in mourning for seven days after the funeral, which was supposed to take place the day after the death. But it was a few weeks before they were able to get the bodies and bury her parents. Aunt Ruthie explained to her that there was a man called the Medical Examiner who had to investigate the murders and that included finding the bullets that killed them. She remembered the shell casing she stepped on and filed another plan in her brain, studying forensics so she could figure out how these guys got away without even being detected and then catch them. With her fists clenched, she swore to herself over and over that she would find her brother and sisters and the murderers if the detectives did not hurry up and get the job done.

———

Rachel felt the plane slowing a bit and getting lower. The stewardess came on the intercom and asked everyone to return to their seats, buckle their belts, raise the trays, and bring back their seats to an upright position. She said they were about to land in New York. The plane shuddered as it passed a cloud cover. Rachel's hearing picked up the strain of the wings and the hydraulics of the wing extenders that were used to slow the plane down as it landed. She heard a ping, and the public announcement sounded, "Prepare for landing, please." She saw a stewardess pull open one of the jump seats and put on her seatbelt. She noticed that the stewardess had two belts, one across her lap like her own belt and one across the chest like a car seat belt. She wondered why the stewardess had a different belt; did it mean that she and the other passengers were less safe? As they cleared the cloud cover, the whole of Manhattan suddenly came into view. She had never seen anything like it. The closest thing in her experience was a four-sided picture called a hologram. Yes! it looked just like a hologram except it was the biggest hologram she had ever seen, and it was real. She actually recognized some of the buildings from pictures and movies. There was the Empire State Building and the United Nations, and the Manhattan Bridge or was it the Brooklyn Bridge? She knew that they were next to each other. She just did not know which came first and which came second.

The big plane glided in, the wings adjusting every now and then. It was a little bit like being on a carnival ride. Her aunt was arranging her hair and looking in a tiny mirror, checking her lips and her eyes. She wondered if she was supposed to do that, too. She had a lot of stuff to learn as a future woman. Even her teacher Robin, who she thought was gorgeous, was very fussy when it came to her eyes and her lips, always checking them before she left. She felt the wheels come down and felt the plane slow down. The cars below got bigger and bigger. The ground was coming up really fast now. She felt and heard almost at the same time the wheels hitting the runway. Immediately, she was thrown back and heard a rush of air outside as the huge engines reversed, and the plane put on its brakes. The stewardess asked everyone to remain seated as the plane taxied to the gate and announced gates for travelers who were continuing on. She was so engrossed with the view outside, she actually blocked all other thoughts out. Wow, she mouthed, no sound coming out, I am in New York, the big city.

She wondered what life would be like here when all of a sudden she felt her throat tightening as she thought about her father and mother and Heather and Karen and Johnny. Tears started rolling down her cheeks and she shook without meaning to. Her aunt saw her beginning to cry and immediately put her arm around her, "I know it's hard to go to a new place, but I will be there for you." Wow, she thought, Aunt Ruthie always knew what to say. She was such a nice person. She never really knew her that well before. She only saw her a few times and didn't really spend any time with her. I guess I am lucky to have her, she thought.

The plane finally stopped at the gate and as if someone blew a whistle at a race, everyone stood up at once to get their carryon luggage out of the bins, crowding the plane's aisle. She stood up on the seat; they were sitting in the first row so only the big seats, which her aunt said was first class, were ahead of them. As everyone stood and took stuff out of the compartments, she froze as her eyes came across a man in the first-class section. His back was to her as he was taking his luggage down. The hairs in the back of her neck stood up. She knew he was one of the men who came into her house. It was sort of a combination of intuition and recognition. She had not even seen his face yet. Nevertheless, she knew that he was there at her house. As he took a briefcase down from the overhead compartment, he looked around at her, not directly, but sort of under his raised arms. Their eyes met and she was sure now, it was Ishy, no doubt about it. He obviously did not think that she could know him, since he did not avert his eyes as their eyes met. He slowly turned around and started walking out.

Rachel literally jumped over her aunt who was in the first seat and ran around her and through some of the passengers to get ahead and near Ishy. As he walked out, he said to the stewardess at the door, "Thanks, it was a nice flight." Now there was no doubt at all in her mind, it was his voice. It was that same Arabic accent, IT WAS HIM!

She waited at the door for her aunt, and when she got

there, she excitedly pointed in the direction of Ishy, or more accurately in the direction where he was, since he had now disappeared down the walkway. Her aunt must have thought that she was pointing to where they needed to go; and while smiling at the stewardess, a smile that said "Isn't my niece cute," she said to Rachel ,"I know," while flashing a side glance at the stewardess. "I know we go this way." Rachel took her aunt's arm and started to pull her to go faster, but her aunt was not moving. It was like the time her neighbor let her walk her dog. She wanted to go one way, but the dog did not want to move. Her aunt pulled back. "What is the matter with you, Rachel?" she asked. "We will get there, we don't have to rush. We will have to wait for the luggage anyway." She explained that the luggage always took a while because they had to unload it from the plane and then bring it to the carousel. Rachel relaxed a bit, she hoped that Ishy had luggage, too. That way she would be able to point him out to her aunt. Her heart was beating fast and her brain was working even faster. What was he doing here? Does he live here? Is he following her? They knew she existed, she realized. She remembered they were looking for her in her room. That night always played like it was a movie, replaying in her mind. She knew that had they found her they would have kidnapped her, too. Is that why he was here? She recalled as if a tape was playing in her mind. *"Yaya, there is no one in her room. Where is the girl?"* She even heard the thick accent in her brain as Ishy said, *"Her bed was not slept in."* And it was Yaya who said, *"The girl must have slept out, if her bed was not slept in. "Salim will not be happy." "Stop talking stupid, Ishy, before we wake the boy up! Let's do what we came here to do, and get out. We will worry about the girl later."*

Why would Salim not be happy? What did he mean, "We will worry about the girl later?" Did they want her too, now? Why? What did she or her family do to them? What did she have of theirs? What did any of them have to do with them? If her father did something to them, why did they want to take all of them? And there were two other names, she tried to concentrate hard, and then another bit of conversation came to her. After she heard Karen scream, one of the men said to the other; *"I wonder what happened over there? Raja can never do anything quietly. Saud should be watching him."* A feeling of deep sadness overcame her as she saw Karen in her mind's eye, recalled her screaming, and realized that they might have hurt her before they took her. Was Ishy here now to take her? She was not so sure now that she wanted to confront him without alerting her aunt to the danger she sensed. Her poor aunt had no idea what she was in for. Then she realized that she did not know what she was in for either. How could she defend her aunt, her uncle, and herself from these people? With a growing sense of uneasiness, she walked alongside her aunt to the baggage area.

CHAPTER 4
BARUCH GLICK

Baruch Glick (Baruch means Blessing in Hebrew), Leo's father, was born in Austria. Baruch's father, Leo's grandfather, was a traveling salesman who died when Baruch was five years old. Baruch was the youngest of nine children and his mother was a strict parent. He was a handsome young man with beautiful hazel eyes, wavy hair, and an athletic body. He was only about five foot five inches, yet he was a great field hockey player, a rough game. He played for a Jewish sports club in Vienna. Before Hitler came to power, the Jews were thriving in Germany, Austria, Poland and in many other European countries. They had their own houses of worship, social clubs, and sports clubs. As a member of the Jewish Field Hockey team in Vienna, Baruch and the best players from all the Jewish clubs in Austria traveled to Palestine for the second Jewish Olympics, called the Maccabiah Games.

Baruch's team came in third; and when the games were over, he and many members of his team decided not to return to Austria. Many of the Jewish athletes from other European countries remained in the country illegally, as well. The athletes knew that Hitler was at the gates, and the Austrian government would be a partner to his designs since he was an Austrian by birth. They took a chance and stayed in Palestine, even though they realized they might wind up in prison or be sent back home to Austria to an unknown and dangerous future.

Baruch left his sweetheart Meira behind, but he wanted to bring her to Palestine to join him. Her parents owned a restaurant where he ate often; and Meira and her sister, Clara, were the waitresses. Both were petite and very pretty. Meira was more athletic, and Clara was more outgoing. The British were extremely strict and did not allow the Jews to enter from Europe. Baruch was trying to bring Meira to Palestine so that they could be married, but it was not an easy thing to do. As luck would have it, Clara was going out with a boy named Zalman Meir who was studying in Vienna. Zalman was born in Palestine; and as a Palestinian-born Jew, he was permitted to marry abroad and bring his bride home. He fell in love with Clara and wanted to bring her to Palestine. She loved him, too, though he was the opposite of Baruch. Zalman was heavy set and had a limp from a motorcycle accident he had as a youth. Zalman was a good-looking young man and very charming; and Clara wanted to marry him and come with him to Palestine, but she had a minor condition. Zalman had to arrange first for Meira to be brought to Palestine so she could marry her sweetheart, Baruch. Zalman, having no other options, married Meira, took her by boat to Palestine so she could marry Baruch. Of course, he had to divorce her first in Palestine and then return to Vienna to marry Clara and bring her back to Palestine, as well.

Many Jews snuck in on ships, the most famous of which was the "Exodus." Baruch would often volunteer to help the Jewish migrants get off the ships. The ships would come as close to the shore as they dared, avoiding sand bars and sharp rocks. Sneaking in at the dark of night off the coast of Tel Aviv and other towns, the ships would drop anchor some distance out. At night they would come closer to the shore and drop off as many passengers as they could before the British discovered them. The beach was too shallow for a ship to come in all the way; there was always a substantial distance to cover. They would either go out in boats to rescue the passengers or, on occasion, if the sea was really calm, they would make a human chain from the ship to the shore and pass the passengers and their small bundles from one to the other. The British, who were in control of the land, would patrol the shore. It was a cat and mouse game with the patrols. They either would keep the passengers from leaving the ship or, if they made it to shore, they would arrest them and keep them in holding pens.

After Baruch's children, Ruth, Leo, and Martha were older, he would tell them stories about how they used to trick the British, give them false information, or make a long chain in the water to nowhere. The British, seeing a chain in the water, would assume that they were bringing in passengers from a ship. They would concentrate on that area, hiding, to catch the passengers as they came ashore. In the meantime, the ship would be elsewhere letting the Jewish passengers off the ship safely. The British soldiers were so serious when on duty that they would never even crack a smile. In uniform it was always duty first; and no matter how harsh the orders, it was not for them to question. Not so when they were off duty. They could be really fun-loving, especially when they drank, which they did regularly. Baruch apprenticed as a furrier in Vienna. In those days, if you did not go to a university, you acquired a profession or a skill by working as an apprentice for several years. Most often, it was without pay, or very little pay, in the employ of an established vocational businessman. Baruch apprenticed as a furrier. It was a good vocation in Vienna but was a lousy one in hot and mostly humid Palestine.

So, Baruch learned how to mix drinks and became a bartender. He had an amazing memory, and he easily learned how to mix drinks and how to speak English and Hebrew. He always loved magic and was fairly good at it, so he was one of the British soldiers' favorite bartenders. He loved taking their money and was always betting them that he could find a card they chose after he destroyed it. They would pick a card which he somehow managed to make them pick, and then he asked them to burn the card, flushing the ashes down the drain. That was when the betting began and, of course, he would get a bunch of them involved. He would climb a ladder to reach the top shelf and would come down holding a playing card in his hand. He would ask them what the card was that they picked. He would tell them that their card was not destroyed, it was in his hand. After some more teasing and maybe even more betting, he would reveal the card in his hand with a big to do and make some extra money. They would offer him a fortune to tell them how he did it, but he would only smile. He knew they would be back and drop their shillings in his pockets again. He made more money with his card tricks than from bartending. The more the soldiers drank, the more they bet.

He especially enjoyed tricking them the night after they helped take the poor refugees off the ship. He could not understand how the British could keep the Jews from entering Palestine. The Jews, who knew by then that they were in very big danger from the Nazis, wanted to come to their ancient homeland. The British saw themselves as the righteous ones, but Baruch and many of his fellow immigrants felt they had as much blood on their hands when it came to Jews being murdered as the Nazis. By not letting their families or friends join them in Palestine, the Jews they intercepted and sent back to Europe were taken off the ships and later sent to concentration camps where they were murdered by the Nazis.

It was personal to Baruch. His wife's parents, who lost the restaurant they owned, initially escaped Austria. They traveled in constant danger first to Switzerland where they were denied entry, then to France where they settled in Paris. They miraculously got passage on a ship heading to Palestine; but while at sea, a British warship intercepted them. When they found out that Jews were onboard with Palestine as their destination, they made the ship go back to France and his parents were returned to Paris. The Nazis, who later advanced into France, located them with the help of the Vichy collaborative government; and they were loaded into trains like cattle and "shipped" straight to a concentration camp. Baruch blamed the British, as well as the Germans, for their death.

Every now and then, Turkish planes would fly over and

drop a couple of bombs as if to say, "Hey, there is a war going on." The Jews of Palestine were keenly aware of the war but from a different perspective. Many felt guilty because their loved ones were in concentration camps, dead, or lost somewhere in the countries where they took refuge. If one actually knew what happened to their relatives, friends, and neighbors, they were considered lucky. Not knowing their fate was almost worse than finding out they perished. The sisters, Meira and Clara, lived totally different lives. Clara and Zalman had one child, a son named Saul, while Meira and Baruch had three children, Ruth, Leo, and Martha.

Leo Glick was born in Tel Aviv, the coastal city of Israel, located in the Middle East. Actually, when he was born it was 1942 and it was still known as Palestine. He was born towards the end of World War II; and while the area was not a dangerous or active area of the war, it was controlled by Britain. Britain was always in the area; but with the discovery of oil in Persia, today's Iran, they formed an Anglo-Persian Company in 1909 in a close relationship with the Shah, its ruler. In 1916 they made a secret agreement with the French and the Russians to divide the Middle East into three areas of influence but leaving the Holy Land to be jointly administered by the three powers. In 1917 the British made a promise to prominent Jews in England that they would look favorably on a Jewish State being formed in Palestine. It went back on promises made to Arab allies and set up a conflict between Arabs and Jews and a strict policy by the British of how many Jews could settle in Palestine. The British also had close relations with trans-Jordan and Saudi Arabia where they had supported years earlier two brothers who became the monarchs of the two countries.

Leo was a happy kid and a smart one, too. When he started pre-kindergarten, he learned Hebrew; and Baruch constantly taught little Leo English. He must have had his father's genes because he picked up languages like it was food. He was trilingual before he was four and could converse in four languages by the time he was six. The children's first language was German. Baruch and Meira hoped that their parents would make it through the war. They wanted the children to be able to talk to their grandparents. As it turned out, their parents did not survive.

Most children did not have grandparents. Baruch once took Leo to the bar, and the British soldiers got such a kick from the little "Jew" boy who could speak English that he helped his dad to make double the tips that night.

CHAPTER 5

LEO AND SALIM

Leo was five when he met Salim. Zalman and Clara had a home in a town near Tel Aviv called Ramat Gan. They also had a vacation home, a beautiful house that Zalman purchased in a town called Gedera which was near a small Arab town called Qatra. During the British Mandate, Gedera became a popular resort due to its mild climate and fresh air. While the relations between Arab villages and Jewish villages and settlements were often strained, the Jews in Gedera and the Arabs in Qatra seemed to get along most of the time.

Zalman was a real estate broker and was doing very well in those days. Arabs mostly owned the land or claimed they owned the land; records were very sketchy and had to be researched so that ownership could be established and the lands sold with a good title. Zalman was able to work in both worlds comfortably since his parents and his grandparents were born locally. Zalman lived near and among the Arabs, spoke their language, knew their habits and ways, and therefore was a logical choice to perfect their title and then sell their land. The Arabs were mostly subsistence farmers or herders. The money they got from the land sales was like manna from heaven, and many of them continued to work the land for the new owners. They did not trust European Jews, and they could not communicate with them. Not only was their language strange, their manners were very foreign, as well. They were brash, direct, and aggressive. They were impatient and excitable. Zalman spoke their language, knew their manners, and was therefore trusted by them. For the settlers, getting a good title was important since much of the land was basically unmarked large tracts of land without borders. Zalman often traveled to Austria to arrange for sales or study. He was doing very well indeed. Clara traveled abroad with Zalman often, a very expensive luxury at that time. She had a nurse for her son and a maid and cook for the house, and Zalman had a chauffeur. They were all local Arabs who worked for pittance. Obviously, not everyone in what was then Palestine lived harshly.

The sisters got together often; and on some occasions in the summer, Meira would pack up a suitcase and travel with the children to Gedera for a week or more. Baruch would usually stay behind, and Leo would spend most of his time with his cousin Saul and the neighborhood kids, both Jewish and Arab. He loved it there; it was total freedom. His mother, his Aunt Clara, and his sisters would stay together; and Leo would get to roam the countryside.

He first met Salim in Gedera. Salim was five also, and the two of them would always compete. Most of the time, Saul, who knew all the local kids, would find a way to instigate a competition. "Hey, Salim, bet you can't outrun my cousin," he would shout. Salim would stick out his chest and say, "No one beats me." And so, all the kids would congregate on the road. They would set up a beginning point and an end point for the sprint and then race. Initially, Leo would always win; but Salim and his friends made the distance longer and longer. Eventually, it was beyond Leo's sprinting abilities. Salim, who was more of a distance runner, began winning. It defined their relationship for the future.

Leo would always start out ahead; but inevitably, Salim would find a way to manipulate the race or the argument or whatever they were competing about that would allow him to win. Zalman's house had a magnificent tree on the property. One of Salim's favorite dares was who could climb the tree higher. It was on one of those occasions that Salim got to the top of the tree first, while Leo was still on his way up. Salim now on his way down, called to Leo who was still climbing and below him, "I will get down faster than you." Leo turned around to climb down; but as Salim hurried down the tree limbs past him, one of the branches that was sticking out scratched his throat and caused an ugly gash. Salim got hurt and was bleeding; blood covered his shirt. It was the only time that Leo saw him scared. It was not the scratch or the blood, Salim said his mom would spank him because he got the shirt bloody. Later, he was proud of his scar. It was like a badge of honor.

Salim was the most competitive boy, Muslim or Jewish, that Leo had ever met. He was always talking about how rich he was going to be. "I will be richer than the King of Jordan, richer than even Rockefeller or Rothschild," he would boast. The rest of them had never even heard these names, but Salim must have heard them somewhere. He knew they were rich, and he knew he was going to be richer. Leo could now carry on a simple conversation in four languages. After one summer in Gedera, he picked up Arabic, as well, while still conversing in German with his parents.

Shortly after Leo celebrated his sixth birthday, Israel, The Jewish State, was formed; and he became an "Israeli." He was a little boy, but he danced in the streets with his sisters and parents. The celebration was such a big deal that he and his sisters could stay up past midnight. He never saw his father so excited. It was bittersweet. Shortly thereafter, seven Arab countries declared war on the new state, His father, Baruch, had to join the Army; and life was never the same again. The trips to Gedera stopped. It was too dangerous. Leo found out that the house at Gedera was practically the border, and his uncle and family could no longer go there safely. Those summer trips stopped. When Leo asked Zalman about Salim, who lived in Qatra, Zalman told him that Salim was now on the other side of the newly-established border. Unbeknownst to Zalman, Qatra was taken over by the Israeli army; and all the Arabs that lived there were gone.

The war that followed the declaration of the state of Israel was fought mostly on the borders. The only exception was Jaffa, a port city next to Tel Aviv. Leo remembered one occasion when a couple of Egyptian planes and an Israeli plane got into an aerial battle over Tel Aviv. They all ran out to the street to watch. It was unbelievable that Israel had a plane; they did not know that it existed. Apparently, the Egyptian pilots did not know that either because when they saw the plane with a Jewish star on it, they were surprised and flew off. The crowds in the street cheered as if the war was won which, of course, it was not. It would take nine months, three weeks, and two days for the war to end.

Baruch was finally home and safe, but life somehow felt different. Leo thought of Salim often. When he saw his uncle, he would ask about Salim and the other boys. Zalman would only say, "They are the enemy now. They are on the other side of the border." Slowly, that summer became a distant memory.

When Leo was twelve, Baruch, who was now working for the Israeli Government, came home extremely upset. He was working for a branch of the Army that looked after the sick and wounded soldiers. It seems that he found out that his supervisor was stealing. His superior would take some of the food and supplies that were ordered for the sick and recovering soldiers and would sell them on the Black Market. Baruch was an idealist. He could not bear to see the soldiers cheated out of the quality food and personal supplies ordered for them. He reported what he observed to his superior's boss; but instead of being thanked and rewarded, he was treated as a troublemaker and was transferred to the remotest facility the Army had in the north and given a menial, humiliating job. It was too much for him to bear, so he decided to leave his beloved Israel and move to America.

It was extremely hard in those days to leave Israel and even harder to get a visa to enter America, but Meira had relatives in Cincinnati; and they made the arrangements to bring the family there. Moving to the States was the worst thing that could have happened to Leo. He was planning to finish school and go to the Israel's Defense Forces like his dad did during the war, and after serving, join and work in one of the collective settlements. Instead, he had to leave all his good friends behind and was going to a school where he had to talk and read and write in English. His thick Israeli accent made everyone tease him and make fun of him.

Leo, with his language skills, quickly mastered English. Not only did he master the language, he worked on and got rid of most of his accent, as well. He was still speaking German at home since it was his parents' preferred language. He also retained Hebrew, mainly by keeping up some correspondence with his friends and by going to mainly Israeli-oriented Jewish summer camps. In high school, he chose French as his language and added another language to his four.

It was the most exciting day of his life when he received the letter that told him he was accepted to the Hebrew University in Israel. It was now considered a world-class university, and he could not wait to get back to Israel. His parents were not very happy with him leaving, but they could not change his mind. They decided to move back to Israel with his sisters, as well. Ruth, Leo's sister, was not happy about leaving the United States. She was studying to be a therapist in New York and was going out with a nice boy named Joe Mintz. Ruth decided to stay in New York and marry Joe. Martha, the youngest, was sickly. She moved and made the trip to Israel with her parents.

As Leo turned eighteen, he and his family were back in Israel. Leo with hazel eyes like his dad and handsome features, was of a modest height. He also inherited his father's athletic build. His hair was blonde and straight, and he was fair skinned, not a good thing in a very hot and sunny country. Leo was enrolled with a science scholarship. He would have preferred to study languages; but the university was looking for science students so he accepted that major, figuring he could minor in languages. After all, to him Hebrew was still a foreign language since he enrolled from America; and Arabic was almost a must in Israel now. Leo had a special deferment from the Israeli Army. In Israel, all 18-year-old males had to serve three years and all females two years. On occasion, a deferment was granted especially for science students and other study fields the government felt was important and wanted their citizens to become adept in. Since everyone born in Israel was a citizen for life unless they renounced their citizenship, they were subject to army service unless they received a deferment while going to the university, which Leo did.

Israel was a totally different country now. He left as a young man; now he found the country to be more modern, yet still unique. It seemed to be a mixture of Middle Eastern, European, and American cultures. On the first day of school as Leo sat down at his desk, a student walked in with an awfully familiar face. He noticed a very prominent scar on his throat. He tried to recall that face. He was of middle height like himself, an athletic body, and a handsome and very tanned face with dark black eyes. The young man was obviously an Arab. He was very self-assured as he strode to a desk near him. Their eyes met, and he could tell that the young man recognized him also but could not place him either. At a break, they both stood up and got close to each other. They both said, almost in the same instant, "Salim!" "Leo!" then they both started laughing. It was truly amazing, both of them recognized each other at the same time. It was as if they were friends their whole life. While they were really friends, hanging out together for only one summer and always competing with each other, after thirteen years, they somehow both remembered that they had been the best of friends.

When Leo asked Salim how a Palestinian from the other side of the border could go to the Hebrew University, Salim told him that just before the war started, his family hid in Gedera which wound up under the control of Israel. He and many thousands of Arabs wound up in Israel and became citizens. He told him that many Arabs, both Muslim and Christian, go to school here and in many other cities. He told him that his parents had died, and his family went to live in Jordan with other members of the extended family. He decided to stay because he thought he had a better chance to succeed in Israel than in Jordan. They were equal citizens in every way except that they did not have to serve in the army. They were represented in the government as elected offi-cials, they were judges, professors and participated in all aspects of the country. They were still discriminated against when it came to housing and in other ways, but he said they had it much better than their brethren on the other side.

CHAPTER 6

ANIMALS TO HUMANS

Over the next three years Leo and Salim truly became best of friends. They both pursued a science curriculum; and just like when they were kids, they were still very competitive. In their third year, they were both assigned to Professor Dan Gill who was a professor of genetics, an extremely hot topic in those days. While Professor Gill was very involved in classroom instruction, he also had a research lab. When on his own, he tended to be fascinated with the human brain and how to maximize human senses and skills. Professor Gill was not only fascinated with the capacity of the brain but also with the limitations of the human's senses as compared to other species. Like many scientists, Gill believed that humans use only a small portion of their brains. He believed that humans could do much better intellectually if they unlocked the brain's potential. One area he was interested in was the abilities of some autistic children and adults. There were many amazing feats by some, especially in memorization and calculations. Such people were often called savants. Though savants could be totally normal in all other respects, he often said that people blocked their capabilities by placing limits on what they thought they could do, creating low expectations. He believed that low expectations begat poor performance and mediocre results. He often repeated the words of Theodore Herzl, the man who promoted the idea of returning to the Jewish homeland and creating a modern Jewish state, "If you desire it, then it's not a fable." In short, everything is possible if you believe it is possible.

Professor Gill wanted to understand why a dog's sense of smell was so much better. Some dogs had extremely sharp smelling abilities and were used in many ways by police, military, and the handicapped. Some dogs were specialists, like looking for cadavers even when buried, and others were used to detect drugs. He wanted to understand why the eagle's eyesight was so amazingly sharp that it was able to see a mouse running on the ground while flying up in the sky, how an owl could hunt in the dark, or how a pigeon found its way home, and so on and so on. Knowing that some of these animal abilities were improved over generations of breeding, he decided that he could generate improvements in humans through genetic changes. It was an area that the scientific community did not look kindly on; and actually, in many countries, laws were passed to control and oversee experimentation.

Professor Gill appeared to many like a mad professor, with his tousled white hair, grizzled face, and the ever-present rumpled white lab coat. He was constantly writing notes, but no one suspected that what he was doing was frowned upon and possibly illegal, research on the sly. His lab never looked very neat. He liked to keep parts of the lab in total disarray, like one sees in mad scientist movies. He thought it would make it easier to keep his work from prying eyes, the messier the better. Very few students were allowed into his lab, and fewer still were allowed to get close to the many animals he worked with. He had a private area that had animal cages all over the place and powerful computers, microscopes, and other scientific equipment were everywhere.

Leo and Salim, who were very good students in Professor Gill's class, had many private discussions with the professor about the ethics of genetic experimentation; and both had ambivalent feelings about the attitude of the scientific community. Within a few months, both Salim and Leo became assistants and close to Professor Gill. They soon graduated from tending to the animals and participating in various tests associated with their studies and the reports on the results, to helping the professor with his "special" animals and the genetic experiments he was involved in. None of these experiments were known to the university, nor reported to them; and the two were sworn to secrecy.

Professor Gill was successful, at times, with minor improvements in the senses of a mouse using the traditional method of breeding a male with a female mouse that he determined to have a strong sense of smell. The result was to bring about an offspring with a slightly better sense of smell, when measured against the parents. But when he tried to increase the strength of the sense of smell by crossing traits and capabilities between species, as was his ultimate goal, he failed. He worked with mice, gerbils, raccoons, and very small microorganisms. His main targets were smell, sight, and hearing. Officially, he worked on experiments in the intelligence of animals by putting them through mazes and other traditional methods of measurement and observation. He made some remarkable discoveries in improving the intelligence of his animals, which brought funding for his lab and enhanced his reputation as a researcher; but when it came to his work on gene transfer, he was very secretive and did not want anyone to know of his work and certainly not of any success or lack of success that he had.

The most radical and illegal work Professor Gill was working on concerned a soup of stem cells from different species which carried the genes he believed could create improved senses in the lab animals he worked with. He obtained these cells in various methods, most of which were not simple or easy. He was always trying different combinations of stem cells and tried to acquire stem cells from other species to inject into adult animals, baby animals, and fetuses. His goal was to have a result through an inoculation of what he called his soup.

Professor Gill did have his ethical limitations. Although he felt that unless he could safely elevate his genetic soup to function with humans, his discoveries with animals would be meaningless; but he was far away from human tests that he could justify.

Professor Gill would tell Leo and Salim, "So what if a mouse could see like an eagle or a moose could hear like a dog? If I cannot get humans to acquire these traits, then the program and I are a failure." He believed that the amazing capabilities nature endowed on so many species in the animal world could be attained by humans. His favorite opening to a discussion often was, "Did you know that this animal or creature has the best sense of smell or taste?" or "How about animals that can manufacture poison or kill prey with bacteria like the giant Komodo Dragons of the Galapagos Islands?" Then he would fill their ears with all the amazing things that other species and other animals could do.

One of the reasons Professor Gill was very reluctant to include human tests was the fact that he was keenly aware of the horrendous experiments conducted by the Nazis. He was determined not to ever experiment on humans without the proper permission and oversight. He felt if he made a break-through, then he could report his results and would be allowed to proceed.

Salim and Leo would sometimes sit for hours with a couple of beers and imagine different animal combinations and roar with laughter. "Hey," Salim would say, "imagine if we gave the professor's wife some praying mantis genes. After they made love, she would eat him." They would both laugh hysterically. Or "Imagine if we could give her some cheetah genes. He would never be able to catch her." Ha ha ha, "but only over short distances." Ha ha ha. Eventually, Professor Gill, with his passion, totally sold them on the possibilities. They were allowed more and more into the professor's confidence and began to help with some of the most secret experiments with the so-called soup. They often talked about the possibility of a human expanding his senses. They knew how the professor felt when it came to human experiments, but they were hoping that eventually they would be successful and could reveal that success to the scientific community. Salim would often fantasize aloud about how much money could be made. He would say,

"Imagine a superman, one who could see like an eagle, hear like some dogs, and most importantly, out-think everyone else." He would say, "I bet the Saudi Arabians would give me half their kingdom if I could give their princes such abilities." Leo was very uneasy with that attitude. He did not feel that Professor Gill was doing this work for the potential financial reward. Leo felt that the professor wanted to better humanity. The idea that the end result was to create a superman or woman was not pleasing to him. He suspected it would not be pleasing to Professor Gill, either.

Leo now spoke fluent Hebrew as if he had never left. At the same time, he spoke English like a born American. His Arabic improved immensely. It was truly functional, as was his German and his French. Leo loved languages and was still hoping to pursue language studies. Salim, on the other hand, was all in on science. He loved the lab, the experiments, and the potential that was presented by the work of Professor Gill. Salim's Hebrew was excellent; and he was proficient in Arabic, his birth language, and English. He was comfortable in both Israeli and Arab societies. Both Leo and Salim were dedicated students and received excellent grades.

In their fourth year they both fell in love with Adina, a student at the university. Even though Leo and Salim attended many of the same lectures, as it happened, Adina was not enrolled in any of these classes; and they met her in classes they did not share. As good friends, they shared the fact that they met a beautiful girl and were dating her but did not share her name. They should have gotten a clue when they were never able to get together and double date. It seemed their girlfriends were never available on the same night. It was like one of those silly scenes in movies when they finally discovered the fact that the girlfriend they both gushed about was the same girl. They were talking about their girlfriend, boasting, and trying to outdo and impress each other, as they still regularly did. There were just too many "me too!" moments when they compared their girlfriends. The same name was a very strong clue, pretty, sure, but that could be many girls. Blue eyes, common, British accent, many Israelis studied in England. But when they found out that both girls had a cute beauty mark in the shape of a heart under her chin, they finally realized they were dating the same girl.

Adina was born to an Arab mother who married a British soldier when the British were still in Palestine. Adina was brought up Protestant and was fluent in English, Hebrew, and Arabic. She was beautiful, with jet-black hair and blue eyes. She had the English bearing, always formal and correct. With her dainty looks, it was as charming as it was sexy. Salim and Leo approached this new problem with the same competitive spirit they approached almost everything they were involved in. They decided to compete for the right to date her.

Theirs was an unusual friendship. They were competitive about everything, but they were always able to devise a civil way to compete. It was really something to experience. The Israeli Muslim Arab and the Israeli Jewish boy both called themselves Palestinian. Even that was an argument between them because Palestinian Arabs felt that they were the only ones that were true Palestinians. But Leo was born when the British were still running the show; and in fact, they were the ones who coined the name Palestine, so Leo had a Palestinian birth certificate in English, Arabic, and

Hebrew. Politics was always a hot topic with them. Salim, even though he was an Israeli, felt the Israelis were occupiers; and Leo felt the Arabs who attacked the day Israel was declared a country made their own bed and now did not want to sleep in it. Salim was not a fanatic, or at least so it seemed to Leo. After all, he befriended him; and he was often critical of other Arab countries who did not want to allow Palestinians full rights and kept them in refugee camps. And so they revealed their friendship to Adina who, after being upset and uncomfortable about dating two friends, agreed to allow their competition for her affections and to abide by the results.

CHAPTER 7

COMPETING FOR LOVE

Their competition, after many meetings and discussions, was agreed to. The contest was actually quite simple: each of them could issue a challenge to the other. They would go three rounds; the one who completed the most would be the winner. If they tied after three, they would continue until one of them won. And so, the challenges began. Salim got to go first. Somehow, he came up with a locust, probably from the lab, and challenged Leo to eat it. It had to be one of the most difficult foods Leo had ever consumed. He closed his eyes and placed the crunchy insect in his mouth. He thought he would lose it right then and there; but then he thought of Adina and her beauty and how much he cared for her, and he bit down on the locust and pretended he was eating a very crunchy piece of bread. He chewed and chewed and finally swallowed, washing it down quickly with a bottle of beer. A major burp followed which almost knocked Salim down. Salim was already weak with laughter from watching his friend's struggle with the locust.

Leo had a comeback, though not the most original given Salim's first challenge was a disgusting meal. He took a cup full of worms that were there for some birds they had in the lab, placed them in front of Salim and said, "Bon Appetit," which is what the French say to each other before they eat. Salim did not seem to have much of a problem. He grabbed them one at a time and with a smile swallowed them while they were still wiggling. Salim almost seemed to enjoy it. The only thing that gave away his discomfort was the three glasses of wine he consumed. Leo, though, felt nauseous. As they finished round one, they were both sick to their stomachs and a little woozy from the beer and wine but learned that one man's delicacy was another man's nightmare.

For the second task, Salim dared Leo to drink a shot glass full of blood. They were in the lab and Salim took a bag of blood and poured some into a water cup. It was a small amount, but Leo did not know if he could do it. He tried to pretend that he was in the desert dying of thirst. He heard many stories about desert people, Bedouins, who when about to die from thirst in the desert would kill their horse or camel and drink their blood in order to survive. Still, this was really scary; but he closed his eyes and just downed the tiny cup of blood. He felt himself go limp with disgust, but the deed was done; and he was getting one step closer to winning the affections of Adina. It was not just Adina; he was very competitive with Salim and wanted to win. Salim, of course, was very competitive as well, and wanted to win just as much.

It was now Leo's turn for the second challenge. He

decided to change the direction a bit. He knew he had to get something really good. He challenged Salim to drink a cup of his own urine. He heard of this being done as a normal habit in India and some other countries, and so he did not feel it was unreasonable. To his surprise, Salim just whipped out his hose, grabbed a beaker, urinated into it, and, while still steaming hot, downed it. Leo got queasy; he could not believe how easily Salim did this. Salim just smiled, picked up another bottle of beer, and without a word just downed it.

"Well, friend" he said, "this is the last one. I have to make it good. I want you to inject yourself with a sample of the professor's soup."

Leo thought Salim was crazy. "I can't do that; the soup is not ready for humans; it might kill me," he fumed.

Salim just smirked and said, "Okay, then you lose. I will just go tell Adina." He started swaggering out of the lab.

"Wait, wait," Leo called, irritably, "let me think a minute," His mind was spinning furiously. He did not know if it was the alcohol he consumed or his desire for Adina, his competitiveness with Salim, or his adventurous nature. He started thinking that maybe he would be able to see in the dark, hear from miles away, or be able to use sonar. Then he got paranoid, what if he should grow a tail or become blind? Hell, he could die. At the end, his desire for Adina and his wanting to win, coupled with his curiosity probably fueled by the alcohol, won out. "Okay, I will do it," he told Salim, who immediately loaded a syringe with the soup and handed it to him. Before he could change his own mind, he injected himself in his thigh and pushed the plunger to the hilt. A cold sweat came over him; but he realized it was fear, not the injection. He regretted his impulsiveness almost immediately and let his anger show. "How could you let me do this?" he shouted at Salim.

Salim looked awfully satisfied with himself, "Hey, it's a fight for a heart of a beauty," he said with an amused look.

Leo, who tried to shake off the alcohol, collected himself and quietly and deliberately told Salim, "Now you!"

"Excuse me?" Salim said, still smug and happy with himself. He looked puzzled.

"NOW YOU!" Leo said much louder than he meant to. He did not just want to challenge Salim, he wanted him to have the same fate. Salim flushed, he never expected it. He never thought it through. It never even occurred to him that Leo would dare him with the same challenge. He never even considered it, and now he was stuck.

He said with less bravado than usual, "To be honest, to be honest" he repeated, "I never thought you would do it, Leo." He looked at the soup and back at Leo, and finally, slowly, and with a look of determination said, "I might be brave, but I am not stupid. You can have Adina. There is no woman in the world that I want that bad." With that, he doubled over laughing, leaving Leo stupefied. Leo was left with very mixed feelings. While he felt great that he won, he was totally scared of what he did. Injecting himself with the soup sort of stole the whole sense of satisfaction from him. Leo did not feel it was a victory. He felt that although he had won Adina, the cost might have been too high. Turned out his elation at winning did not last long.

His obvious show of bravery, or was it stupidity, obviously did not impress Adina. When he happily told Adina that he and Salim finished their contest to win the right to date her and that he won fair and square, she laughed heartily. She gave him a hug and congratulated him for his win and then told him that she was sorry but she loved Salim more than him and could not abide by their agreement. He was totally surprised and humiliated when Adina told him that Salim was always her choice, and she could not in good conscious lie to him and date him. Needless to say, the whole episode had a chilling effect on their friendship. Leo resented the fact that Salim had him do something that he found too dangerous to do himself. He also felt that by Salim challenging him with an act that he found so very dangerous for himself, meant that Salim had little regard for his safety. He also resented Adina, given that Salim was willing to give her up, and he showed he cared for Adina more. While he was willing to sacrifice more, she allowed the competition to take place even though she knew that she would renege on her promise to abide by the result of the contest if he won. She planned to go with Salim no matter who won.

Their friendship cooled, and then, adding to the coolness between the friends or maybe because of it, Leo became closer to Professor Gill and seemed to get involved in areas Salim was not invited to participate in. Given that Salim was much more passionate about the experiments in the lab, he felt that he should be the one to be closer to Professor Gill. He resented Professor Gill and Leo for leaving him out.

In their last months at the university working with Professor Gill, Leo became even closer to him. The professor revealed to Leo that while he had very little success with mice and other rodents he injected, he discovered almost by accident that offspring of rodents he injected showed some abilities that were consistent with the soup they injected into their parents. Leo began to work with the professor on following offspring and testing them for special abilities. The results were very random. Some offspring had abilities and some did not. Some had better sight or better hearing, some showed amazing abilities in the maze tests, showing a superior intelligence compared to their siblings. Because the results were so random and inconclusive, the professor and Leo felt that the continuation of the research was not ethical. They could never test humans, given that the results could affect their children and not only affect them but in random and unpredictable ways. For Leo, these conclusions were very scary. He was very worried about what his stupid action of injecting himself could mean to any children he might have someday.

The professor developed some health problems and agreed with Leo that the mutations in the offspring of mice he injected were not consistent with his expectations. He agreed with Leo that it meant that experiments with humans were not likely in the near future. Leo never disclosed to him that he was the first human to be injected with the soup. But these results frightened him and made him promise to himself that he would not have children. Professor Gill decided that without multi-generational controlled experiments, which he did not have the facilities or the funding for, he was unwilling to continue with the special private lab. He asked Leo not to divulge that information to anyone, including Salim. The professor never shared with Salim that some of the mutations passed onto the offspring. He told Leo that he expected to retire soon and close the labs. He did not want to risk anyone else continuing with the experiments, except perhaps him. He asked Leo if he would like to be recommended to replace him.

Leo knew the results of the experiments and was familiar with all aspects of the lab. He could have continued the work; but he was not interested enough in that field, he wanted to pursue his languages. He shared his feelings with the professor who accepted his decision.

Salim was working primarily on the extraction of genes for the various animals they chose, and he sensed that the professor did not want to share the research or the results with him. There was still a distrust of the Arabs in Israel. Even though on the campus the animosity was generally absent, it did not mean that there was complete trust. Salim knew that Professor Gill was not well and that he was planning to retire soon and end his research. He was much more passionate about the prospects of the genetic work and the mutations leading to enhancing the senses of humans. He saw multiple possibilities for fame and fortune that success would bring.

Even though Salim was recruited by Oxford to continue his studies in genetics, he decided to stay and work with Professor Gill. Meanwhile, Leo was offered a position with a university in Cincinnati and was getting ready to return to the United States. It was not an easy decision for Leo. He did not want to leave his parents and his sister Martha, who was sick; but his other sister Ruth lived in New York, on Long Island, and so he had some family in the States.

While he told everyone, including his family, that he would be teaching, in fact he had gotten an offer from the American government's Central Intelligence Agency. They were very interested in his language skills and his knowledge of the Middle East. They wanted him badly and evidently cleared it through the Israeli government to allow him to leave without serving in the Israel Defense Forces, as was required for all Israeli citizens, especially after getting a deferment. When Leo's family migrated to the United States, he became an American citizen; but he was also an Israeli citizen. The United States, a strong ally and provider of the Israeli defense forces, could not be denied; and they managed the Cincinnati University job as a cover for him. The United States government job was to be a secret.

And when the fourth year was done, Leo and Salim graduated, both with distinction. Salim continued to work with Professor Gill and his genetic research. Leo moved to Cincinnati and the CIA, not missing the research but worrying about the injection of genetic soup he stupidly injected himself with. Salim continued his studies and eventually earned his PhD. Several months after receiving his degree, Professor Gill died in his sleep. Salim took over the professor's position in the university, his lab with the genetic research, and he restarted the secret research into altering the genetic makeup of humans. Leo never told the professor or anyone else about that injection. Salim and Adina were the only other people who knew about it.

Time moved on. Salim married Adina and they had a son named Bart. Leo met and then fell in love with April who was a friend of a co-worker at the CIA. He knew he had to share with her that they could not have children. He needed to be honest with her; and if that was a deal breaker, then he would have to live with it. It was very traumatic and humiliating for him to tell her the whole story. He felt if he couldn't trust her with the story, how could she marry him. Finally, when he felt the opportunity presented itself, he explained to her the reason for his reluctance to marry. He told her that he was trusting her with something that no one except for three people knew, about the foolish contest he made to win the right to date a girl. He had to let her know about the secret research so she would fully understand how idiotic an act it was. He told her how after he challenged his friend to the same act, his friend laughed at him and that the girl wound up laughing at him, too. She told him she had no intention of going with him, she loved his friend. So now he was afraid to have children because he had no idea what he did to himself or his genes. He explained to her that he had no symptoms but was afraid that there could be a mutation in the next generation. She listened to him with a mixture of surprise and disapproval, but she truly loved him and was very sympathetic and understanding. She could understand why he decided to discontinue his work with genetics. She said they would take it one step at a time and would figure it out.

They married and after a few years and much encouragement by April, Leo eventually relented and agreed to take a chance and have a child. When Rachel was born, they watched her like hawks. They saw a healthy, happy baby and did not note any special behaviors or peculiarities. They had Karen two years later, and Heather followed two years after. Two years after that, Johnny arrived, the boy they wanted after three girls, a boy to carry the Glick name. He did not show any special abilities either. They knew that their children were very smart but did not note any other special abilities, maybe because they never looked for them. They did not want to face the possibility that they were affected by Leo's foolish action many years earlier.

Leo never revealed to the CIA his research work at the Hebrew University or his foolish bet. He was afraid that if somehow his children had any of the genes he injected himself with years ago, they would be in jeopardy. He thought they might be sought by Salim or perhaps someone else who he may have told the secret to and would want them as guinea pigs. He worked to keep his children safe and made it clear to his handlers, Adam and Joe, that they must always keep an eye on his family.

Leo worried even more after Salim's world collapsed—Salim changed. Leo felt a cold fury from him. He knew that Salim continued the experimentation and would be working with offspring of the animals he injected. Leo and Salim had little contact until the tragedy that befell them both.

CHAPTER 8

THE LUGGAGE CAROUSEL

As Rachel and her Aunt Ruthie walked to the baggage area, they joined the passengers anxious to get their bags. They hurried down long corridors like it was a race. People tried to get by them from the right then from the left, all in a hurry to wait. The luggage never got to the carousels before the passengers. To Rachel, it seemed that they were part of a river of bodies, flowing downstream. After a while, they came to a down escalator. Rachel was amazed that even on this narrow escalator, people tried to get by. Her eyes were constantly searching for Ishy. She knew it was him; she was positive. As they approached the luggage pickup area, she considered saying something to her aunt. She knew how difficult the whole subject was for her. Then she remembered that she could not say anything; and even when she tried to communicate with her, she could not do so properly. They were now at the end of another long corridor which finally, after another escalator, opened into a giant room with huge circular carousels that were turning round and round with nothing on them. It was a while but then suitcases started to come out of an opening from above, which looked like a big mouth. It was like the mouth was spitting out suitcases and duffle bags and all sorts of packages, which then tumbled down to the carousel and started to go round and round. Then, all of a sudden, she saw Ishy. He had a cart and was loading some bags onto it. They were very long black bags. He then pushed the cart towards the exit. It was then that she saw Yaya on the other side waiting for him. There was no mistake in her mind that it was Yaya. As Ishy got closer to Yaya, they waved to each other.

She moved as close as she dared to them and stood behind a pillar. She strained her ears and listened to them. They spoke in this harsh guttural accent. "So how was your trip?" asked Yaya.

Ishy replied, "It was a little bumpy, but not too bad considering how boring it was. What is new at the Embassy?" Ishy asked.

"Nothing really. Did you find out where they are going?"

"No, no clue. I know they live somewhere on Long Island, but I did not get an address."

"Don't worry, we will just follow them from here."

Ishy said, "Well, let's go. I need a smoke. They won't let you smoke on a plane anymore." They left the terminal through the front doors, leaving Rachel scared, shaken, concerned, and visibly pale, the blood draining from her face. They will follow them? Find out where they live and kidnap her just like Johnny, Karen, and Heather? And what will they do to Aunt Ruthie and Uncle Joe? Will they kill them like they killed her mom and dad? What was she going to do? She had to warn her aunt! She dropped to the floor behind the pole where she was standing and sat there holding her head. She did not know what to do.

"Rachel," she heard somewhere deep in her brain. Then she heard it louder "RACHEL, RACHEL." She stirred and came around like from a trance. She saw her aunt frantically looking around and calling her. She jumped up and ran over to her aunt, hugging her frantically. She was only twelve. How was she going to protect them from these horrible people? With her aunt's arm around her, they went to the baggage carousel together and found their luggage. They loaded their bags on a cart that her aunt had gotten and proceeded to the exit. Once they got through the doors, it was pandemonium again. Aunt Ruth and Rachel looked around and spotted Uncle Joe by the curb, a few cars down from where they stood. Uncle Joe was waiting for them next to his car. He was all business as he took over, taking their suitcases from the cart and loading them into the car's trunk. Rachel loved the car. It was sleek and sporty, red, with a plate that read Eldorado. She squeezed into the back seat with a couple of the small bags that did not fit in the trunk and off they went. Rachel was on her knees looking out the rear window intently watching the cars behind them.

They left the airport and got on a highway called Grand Central Parkway and got off on an exit called Clearview Expressway. She saw a huge stadium and a large electric sign that read "Let's Go Mets" written in big letters across it. It was very cloudy, and it became really dark. While it was late afternoon by now, it was not sundown dark but rather the darkness of a storm brewing. The farther they drove, the darker it got. They passed a sign for the Whitestone Bridge and beyond that a sign for the Cross Island Parkway. Suddenly, as if materializing out of thin air, she saw a black car following behind them with a familiar face driving. It had that little ornament on the hood that she remembered was a Mercedes. The car was not right behind them but perhaps four cars back; but with her keen eyesight, she could tell it was Yaya driving. She could not see the passenger, the other cars obstructed that view; but she knew Ishy must be in the passenger seat. Her body tensed up as she tried to think what she could do. They were keeping their distance, just following them.

It got darker and darker and then it was as if they drove into a car wash. It triggered a memory. She remembered going with her dad to a car wash. She loved staying in the car while it was sprayed with water, then soap, then other stuff, and finally water. It was like the rain now coming down from the sky. Rachel remembered how the water sprayed the car clean, and then the heaters coming on, with a loud noise, kind of like the big plane engines. The kids went with her dad many times, all of a sudden she thought of Johnny, Heather, and Karen. She missed them. They used to love staying in the car as it went through the car wash. Johnny screamed each time another machine came on and sprayed the car. She and her sisters loved it, too, especially the sensation of suddenly being covered by a curtain of water and then when coming out into the clear. Just like now with the rain coming down so heavily, even though Uncle Joe turned on the windshield wipers full blast, they could not see more than fifteen or twenty feet ahead. She stared out of the back window of the car, but it was impossible to see, even for her. She could barely make out the car in back of them, let alone the fourth or fifth car behind them. Maybe we will lose them in this rain, she thought. Maybe they will get lost. She still could not understand how they found her or why they were following. She wanted them gone, but she realized it was just a fantasy or a dream, since the Eldorado had slowed down and was practically crawling along.

The rain got so bad that Uncle Joe pulled totally off the road. He drove a little while on the side of the road until the Eldorado was under an overpass where there was no rainfall. It was like going through the curtain of water and then suddenly there was no rain on top of them, exactly the same as in the car wash. Rachel was so consumed and concerned with the Mercedes behind them that she could not really appreciate or enjoy the experience. Other cars behind them had the same idea. They followed and parked under the overpass behind them. The rain in front of them and in back of them was still a wall of water, but they were in a dry zone. Cars were still driving by on the highway, raising a spray as they passed. It was eerie to see car after car break through the water curtain, come into the clearing, and then out again into the shower. Rachel followed each car, but she did not see the Mercedes. She was sure it did not pass. She had kept her eye on the road and did not miss a car. Finally, the rain calmed down a bit and turned into a drizzle. She could now see out the back of the car. There were several cars parked behind them, most were not under the overpass. Several cars back, she could now see the Mercedes. She knew for sure that it was them, no mistake about it.

She shrank in her seat so they would not see her and immediately thought how silly that was. They did not know that she knew who they were, but she was sure that they knew that they were driving in a flaming red Eldorado and that she was in it. From her crouched position, she could still see the car; and so she was shocked and amazed to see a black limo pull in behind Yaya and Ishy's car. It looked an awful lot like the limo that had been parked outside her house the morning after she lost her family. Who was that, she thought. Are they the same people or was this just coincidence? She concentrated really hard and saw the doors open on either side of the limo and two men got out. The men walked over to the Mercedes. They were holding what looked like guns in their hands. She watched as they got to the Mercedes. She could see them pointing the guns into the car. She tapped Uncle Joe excitedly on the shoulder, pointing towards the two cars some fifty feet behind. He turned around, patted her on her hand, and said, "Don't worry, the rain eased up so we won't be here but a few more minutes." They can't see what was going on back there, she realized. They cannot see what I see. The two men were getting Yaya and Ishy out of their car and walking them to the limo. They seemed to be walking with their hands behind their back. Then she realized that they were handcuffed. They placed both of them in the back of the limo, and then one went back to the Mercedes and drove off right past them. She saw the other man get into the limo and follow. They slowly drove off back into the rain and away. She wondered if she just imagined the whole thing; maybe it was just wishful thinking.

After a few more minutes, the rain let up almost

completely. Uncle Joe found a break in the traffic and pulled out to continue their trip home. Her mind was like a whirlpool, so many thoughts and emotions were running through her. She had gone from numbing fear to a sense of relief and elation. She was also trying to figure out who the people were who rescued them and arrested Yaya and Ishy. Someone else knows, she thought, SOME ONE ELSE KNOWS WHO THE KILLERS AND KIDNAPPERS ARE!!! Those two men in the limo were angels, she concluded, because she could never convince anyone that she knew the voices or the faces of the killers and kidnappers. Now, she thought, someone else knows. Someone else that will believe her. She tried to convince everyone that she knew, that included all the policemen and women who questioned her. It included her Aunt Ruthie, Uncle Joe, and Robin. She knew it was not a coincidence. Somehow she knew that their rescue just before was connected because she remembered the limo and the two men in dark glasses leaning against it on that terrible morning. Realizing now that someone else knew filled her with hope. Rachel felt that if someone else knew about these guys, maybe they also knew where Karen, Heather, and Johnny were.

That idea filled her with a sensation of relief that she had not felt since she first accepted that her whole family was gone. And there was another feeling welling up inside her, a feeling of revenge. She swore that she would somehow find the killers and kidnappers, but first she would have to find out how they found her and who arrested them. It was obvious to her that it was not the police. It must have been some other agency or entity, so what now? How is she going to find these men? She also wondered if the others would come after them now. She knew there were three more killers out there. Would they find her? Maybe they would not find out that Ishy and Yaya were arrested. She was getting exhausted from all these thoughts and emotions and slowly closed her eyes and let sleep overtake her.

CHAPTER 9

LIFE WITH AUNT RUTH

Rachel's life in New York changed dramatically. Her Aunt Ruth took her to the best doctors who confirmed that her vocal cords were intact and offered no physical reason for her inability to speak. The doctors found her hearing to be phenomenal, and her eyesight was off the charts. She was referred to a psychiatrist specializing in traumatic psycho-trauma and who was proficient in sign language. She underwent a lot of tests, including mental and intelligence tests. The conclusion was that she has amazing hearing and vision. She also had an excellent sense of smell and taste and, above all, a very quick mind with a photographic memory and, therefore, total recall abilities.

Aunt Ruth engaged a private sign language tutor for the three of them. Rachel, of course, picked it up much faster than did Aunt Ruthie or Uncle Joe.

West Hempstead, a town in Long Island close to the New York City borough of Queens and a little more than 40 minutes from Downtown Manhattan, was known for their excellent special education in their schools. Rachel was not only quickly mainstreamed, she was also placed in the gifted program. After several months in school, it seemed that Rachel was learning so quickly that she was bored in class, even with extra work. She would often be off with her thoughts. Her test results were always an A or A+. She never got anything wrong. On a couple of occasions, her math teacher marked an answer wrong; and she would prove to her that her answer was right. The same thing happened with history. Her photographic memory impressed her teachers; they had never seen such a display of recall before in a child as young as Rachel. While appearing to be sort of dreamy when she was off in her thoughts, Rachel seemed to hear everything and never missed a thing. She still kept mainly to herself, but on occasions would join the other children in play. Rachel also joined the chess club, and soon even the teacher in charge of the club could not beat her.

The most amazing thing was that she did not have to communicate verbally. She rarely used her sign language, and most of the students and some of the teachers forgot that she couldn't talk. Her teachers told Aunt Ruth that they thought she should place Rachel in a school for gifted children or at least supplement her studies at home to accommodate her superior intelligence. Her aunt, of course, had already been doing that with the Sign Language teaching; and Rachel, being a voracious reader, always had a book in her hands. Girls always matured faster than boys, but Rachel seemed to be more mature at twelve than many adults. Her loss had a lot to do with her sad look, and it was hard to even get a smile out of her. Her favorite books had to do with forensics and crime novels, and she loved the computer that her aunt bought her. It was the finest computer money could buy, and Aunt Ruth did her best to keep her busy at home. Rachel discovered that she had a special affinity for languages. Aunt Ruthie told her that she was just like her father. She could actually learn a language from the computer programs, simply by memorization. West Hempstead had a very diverse population; it was a lot more diverse than in Cincinnati. The town had a Muslim family originally from Iran, and several of their young children were in her classes. She was very curious about the Muslim religion and the Arabic culture and learned a lot about it, including some of their holidays, culture, and even some of the language.

Rachel loved her computer and found that she could type faster than she could write long hand, legibly that is. There was a special place in her brain that continued to go over the events in her house. She still had no idea why these men attacked her family, kidnapped her siblings, and evidently tried to get her, too. She was always looking over her shoulder in case anyone wanted to kidnap her or harm her aunt and uncle. She read the newspaper every day, especially scanning for police and crime stories, as well as the news feeds on the internet. She even was able to view police scanners by finding their signals and listening in. Her aunt hated to talk about that night and always discouraged Rachel from talking about it. She did not refuse to discuss it; however, if Rachel brought it up. It was as if a faucet was turned on and she would become teary eyed. As tears would run down her cheeks, she would shake her head and say that she couldn't make any sense out of the whole thing. She said she was constantly in touch with the police in Cincinnati and the FBI; but so far, they had no clues.

Rachel would write down for her what she was doing on the computer. She tried to communicate with her using sign language about the events as she experienced them, but her aunt would just cry and say some psychological mumbo jumbo. "That night was very traumatic for you, and sometimes we just imagine things when we are very stressed." She would tell her how thorough the police were and recount to her all the reasons why they had not made progress so far. "They don't have clues, there are no cameras in the area that caught the killer/kidnappers. I am calling all the time, and they tell me they are working on it." For some unexplained reason, Rachel never told her aunt about the limo and the two men she had seen leaning on it outside the house. When she told her aunt about the black Mercedes and what happened at the airport and on the ride home, her aunt thought it was her imagination. She thought that to add the fact that she had seen that limo before would be just as doubtful to her aunt, if not more.

Rachel learned how to do research at the school's library and with her computer. She found newspapers of the day that they arrived in New York from Cincinnati. She scoured the newspapers and found nothing about two men arrested on the highway. While she knew for certain what she saw and never doubted any of her memories on an intellectual level, she questioned at times that maybe it was her imagination, but only when she felt very down and emotional. Rachel thought if only she could find that limo and the men that were in it, they could let her know if they knew something. They obviously knew she was in danger and saved her. More importantly, they must have been following her. Or they were watching Ishy and Yaya? She wondered why no other attempts were made to kidnap her. She wondered if the men in the limo got all the men from that night. Did they know where her siblings were? She always had so many questions in her mind. Where were her mom and dad buried? Why couldn't she be at the funeral? And what about her brother and sisters? Were they alive? Where were they? She often felt that there were things about her dad that she did not know and that she must find out more about him in order to find Karen, Heather, and Johnny. Rachel often asked her aunt what happened to her parents' belongings. Her aunt told her that the house and contents were sold, and all of her parents' money and the money they got for the house and everything else that was sold, was placed in a trust for her. Her aunt told her that she slowly was becoming a very rich young lady. "Your stocks are doing extremely well," she would say, "and one day we might have to borrow from you. Ha! Ha!" She told Rachel that she had kept all her mother's jewelry for her, as well as a few heirlooms from her grandparents, who died in a car accident along with her Aunt Martha.

Rachel was not really interested in the possessions. She wanted to see all the papers her father had, at least the ones that were not taken by the killers/kidnappers. She knew that if she was going to find Johnny, Karen, and Heather, she needed to look for clues. Maybe they would give her something to go on, or at least a hint at a reason for what happened. Her aunt told her that all of her father's and mother's papers, letters, and so on were taken by the police; and they still had it all as far as she knew. Rachel did not let up and kept bugging her aunt to get the stuff. When her aunt tried, the police told her that the FBI and their people were still holding the papers for their investigation.

Rachel's thirteenth birthday was approaching. In the Jewish religion, when a girl is twelve, she is Bat Mitzvahed; and when a boy is thirteen, he is Bar Mitzvahed. In Hebrew, Bat means daughter of, and Bar means son of; Mitzvah means commandment. Literally, and by rules of the religion, it means that the girl or boy are now adults with responsibility for their own sins. Many Jewish families celebrate the girl's Bat Mitzvah at thirteen, also. The ceremony is a coming of age ritual that recognizes the boys and girls as adults before God and the congregation. It takes place in a special religious ceremony, after which the boy or the girl become responsible as Jewish adults. They are required to observe all the laws and regulations that the religion requires by the Old Testament and by custom. The children have to recite in the Hebrew language and need to learn how to recite and sing both from the sacred scroll and a passage describing the reading from the bible that day. They also have to sing in the synagogue in front of the whole congregation. It is a really big deal and culminates in a big party which sometimes can resemble a gala as big as a wedding.

Rachel's parents were never big on religion. They considered themselves secular Jews. Secular Jews generally do not follow prescribed restrictions and Sabbath observance. They usually celebrate traditional Jewish holidays as cultural and historical holidays and festivals and adhere generally to life-cycle events, such as births, circumcision, marriages, and deaths. Rachel had planned to be Bat Mitzvahed at thirteen, as do many children and their families; and since her parents were not members of a synagogue, they did not mind. Aunt Ruthie and Uncle Joe were not very observant either, but they were members of a synagogue in West Hempstead and would occasionally go and celebrate the holidays in Temple. They wanted Rachel to have the Bat Mitzvah, since her thirteenth birthday approached, just as her parents had planned; but Rachel did not want a Bat Mitzvah. She, of course, could not sing or recite from the bible and had not studied for her Bat Mitzvah. She had read the Bible in English and in Hebrew; and with her affinity for languages, she was able to understand and even read Hebrew. She made it clear to Aunt Ruth and Uncle Joe that she was not interested in having a ceremony. She made it clear to them that until her brother and sisters were found, she would not celebrate. She knew from her readings that traditionally girls were Bat Mitzvahed at 12. She reasoned that since she would be 13, and not 12, then it could be 14 or 15. It didn't matter. Rachel kept insisting that she wanted to wait, but her aunt did not relent either and kept trying to change her mind. They finally compromised, and Rachel agreed to have a token ceremony in Temple; and Aunt Ruth and Uncle Joe agreed to skip the party afterwards and have a big celebration when they found Johnny, Karen, and Heather.

For her religious ceremony, Rachel wrote an essay which she presented to the congregation by using sign language. Reading in different languages in her head was a snap, but signing was a different challenge. It turned out that signing was not an international language. It had variations in every language. While Rachel could now read English, Hebrew, and a little bit of Arabic, she only learned the English sign language, so she signed her essay in English. Her aunt read it aloud as she signed. The congregation was very appreciative of her efforts, and she was rewarded with applause, a song of celebration, and a shower of candies that they threw in her direction, a tradition.

It was all bittersweet for Rachel, and she could not enjoy the celebration. Aunt Ruthie and Uncle Joe wanted to buy her a special gift; they discussed a bicycle or new clothes. Rachel had only one request: she wanted to go back to Cincinnati and look through her parents' papers and other possessions that the police had. That was her only wish.

Right after the ceremony, her Aunt Ruthie gave her an envelope with two airline tickets in it to Cincinnati for the both of them. "It's your birthday wish, so I made some phone calls to the Cincinnati police. They agreed to let you go through the papers. They are kind of strict about who they allow access to. From their point of view, they are still looking for the murderers and kidnappers. They said they have to keep a chain of custody on all the papers. After checking with the FBI, they called and said they would accommodate us as best they can." Rachel was ecstatic. She hugged Aunt Ruthie and signed, "This is great, how did you pull it off?" Aunt Ruthie said, "Well, I had your psychiatrist write a letter, explaining that this trip was a necessary and important part of your treatment for your traumatic stress." Rachel was overwhelmed. She kept signing over and over, "This is great!, This is great!" She was still signing to herself when she returned to her room. "This is great! This is great!"

CHAPTER 10

THE GIFT

As Rachel's school year came to a close, she got more and more excited about the trip back to Cincinnati. She had been obsessed thinking about what she might look for in her father's papers. She tried to figure out how she was going to look for clues of his and her mom's killers and Johnny, Karen, and Heather's kidnappers if she didn't even know what she was looking for. One thing she knew for sure, somehow, somewhere, there must be something that would give her a start at finding the kidnappers and the murderers. She thanked Aunt Ruth and Uncle Joe over and over for giving her the gift she had wished for. Rachel really loved her Aunt Ruthie and her Uncle Joe. They treated her like she was their own child, and she swore that she would never do anything to hurt them. She knew that the gang that she was after numbered five; and two seemed to be caught by the limo people, whoever they were. She figured that unless she solved the crime, they would all be in danger.

It was a cool July morning. Uncle Joe drove them to LaGuardia Airport in Queens in his red Eldorado. Boy, did he love that car. "The airport is named after a former mayor," she signed to them. They were looking forward, so they did not see her as she traced their route backwards from her trip after arriving a year earlier. It seemed like it was five years ago. As they drove by Shea Stadium where the New York Mets played baseball, there was that sign again: LET'S GO METS over the big stadium. She smiled as they drove by and recalled the first time she saw the sign. She did not know then that her Uncle Joe was a die-hard Yankees fan and that any mention of the Mets would make him crazy. She loved to tease him; and when they passed the stadium, she patted him on his shoulder excitedly and pointed to the stadium. He made some noise she did not acknowledge. She knew now that it was one of two baseball teams in the city. The Yankees were the older team, and fans were either for one team or the other. The fans of one team usually did not tolerate the other. Uncle Joe always said that he would never go to Shea Stadium, even if the tickets were free, unless the Mets were playing the Yankees and then only to cheer the Yankees on.

Uncle Joe dropped them off at the Delta departure gate. They kissed Uncle Joe goodbye and checked in at the sidewalk booth. Her aunt took the baggage tickets, and they went into the terminal and to their gate. Somehow everything now seemed different. Not only was she now taller than Aunt Ruthie, she was not sidetracked by Ishy and Yaya and not as traumatized. She looked at everything so differently. She was a scared young girl when she arrived. Now she was more self-assured, and she was on a mission back to her

Cincinnati. They walked to their gate and took a seat facing the runway. A while later she saw a plane pull up to the long corridor-like contraption, and soon passengers were filing out through the door. Sometime later their flight was announced, and after standing in line for a bit, they boarded. The trip was uneventful. She had a window seat and enjoyed seeing the big city as they took off and flew over it. As they left the sky over the city, she looked at the endless farms, mountains, and forests on the way to Cincinnati. A very nice stewardess came by and gave them snacks and drinks, and an overhead TV screen showed a pretty violent movie she did not care to watch. She closed her eyes and thought about the challenge ahead.

The landing was a replay of her last flight. They landed in the airport that was actually in Kentucky and then rented a car and drove back to the Marriott Residence Inn where they had lived for a while after that terrible night. It was not just a hotel room, but more like an apartment. They called it a suite. The suite had two bedrooms, one for her and one for her aunt. They each had their own bathroom, and there was a kitchenette with a dining area and a living room. It seemed that they were at the hotel only about an hour when the phone rang. "Hi," Aunt Ruthie said. "Sure, that would be great. We can order in some pizza. See you soon."

"Who was that?" she signed.

"You'll see," her Aunt said smilingly. She called a local pizza place called Papa Joes and ordered a mushroom pizza, Rachel's favorite. A half an hour later there was a knock on the door. Her aunt called from her bedroom, "It must be the pizza. There is a twenty on the table. Give the guy a dollar tip and make sure you get the right change." Rachel took the twenty-dollar bill and opened the door. If she was able to scream, she would have. She actually did have her mouth open with her hands over it. There standing in front of her, smiling, stood her favorite teacher, Robin. The pizza guy was right behind her.

As the three of them chomped on the mushroom pizza, they chatted like three old friends. Robin was surprised at Rachel's appearance. She had to look up now to see her face. It had only been a year, but Rachel must have grown four inches. It was a tough adjustment for Robin who was tiny at five foot two, especially since she had Rachel as a student; and while they communicated every now and then, she had not seen her since she left for New York. Rachel, in addition to the surprise of seeing Robin, had another surprise. Robin, who was now teaching a little boy who was born deaf, had learned sign language and could communicate with Rachel without her aunt's help. They dug into the pizza and into conversation, hungry for both. If one entered the room, one would see three women, arms in the air making gestures in an animated fashion. It would seem weird unless one realized that they were communicating in sign language.

Robin, who wanted to know what brought them back to Cincinnati, was stunned to find out that Rachel actually saw the murderers and the kidnappers. She asked a lot of questions, all of which Rachel had heard before. Could she have imagined it? How could she see them in the dark? How did they manage to leave no clues and leave with the doors locked from the inside? After all, Robin recalled, forensics found nothing that would implicate anyone. Robin also remembered reading at the time that there were no footprints from anyone other than the family members. They looked for hairs that people always drop and other clues but found none. Robin wondered aloud, "Does that mean that none of the family or the investigators or the intruders lost any hair? How could they find nothing?"

Rachel pointed out, "Nothing meant nothing they could use." She continued, "so many people trampled around the house that day, I was surprised that they even bothered to look. They would have had to take the DNA of every policeman and detective that was there that night, also workers, landscapers, and anyone else that had a reason to be there," she signed. "Same for footprints and fingerprints." As they spoke, she shared with them her insights. Aunt Ruth and Robin were surprised at Rachel's knowledge of forensics.

Rachel had her own idea why the police had no success. She signed, "Mike, the first policeman on the scene, did not seem very competent. They probably were not looking for hair right at the start when they had the best chance of finding some." Robin wanted to know how she remembered the policeman's name. "I don't know why or how I remember," she signed, "I just do, maybe because in my mind, I reviewed the events of that night so often. I don't want to forget anything about what happened, not the tiniest thing. It might be important in solving this mystery and finding my brother and sisters."

"Well," Robin told them, "I took a week off from school so that I can help you." Rachel clapped her hands happily at the good news. "Ruth told me that you got permission to go through your family's things and figured you could use some assistance. I really want to help."

Rachel looked at both of them, tears welling up in her

eyes as she signed, "I am not sure if we will find something that will help, but just having the two of you help me is a blessing for me." They chatted a while longer and then Robin said her goodbyes. They agreed to meet tomorrow at the police station; and after mutual hugs, Robin left and Rachel and Aunt Ruth went to bed exhausted from the trip and the trip down memory lane with Robin. Recalling the night of the murder was very hard for both of them.

Rachel had a hard time falling asleep; and when she did, it was a restless sleep. She tossed and turned, woke up a few times looking at the clock, hoping that it would be morning already. She was thrilled when some light started coming in through her window. She jumped out of bed and hurried to get washed and dressed.

CHAPTER 11

SALIM AND THE EMBASSY

Salim was sitting at his desk in the Jordanian Embassy in New York City. He was ashen faced. How could this happen? A simple task had become such a debacle. He just received word that Ishy and Yaya would not be returning. They simply disappeared, as well as their car, from the Cross Island Parkway on Long Island. They had satchels full of guns, ammunition, and all sorts of other sophisticated equipment, like night vision goggles and eavesdropping devices. The Embassy security officers, who did not know about the extracurricular activities they were engaged in, were worried about them since there was a lot of hostility towards Muslims in the United States. Before Salim could get involved, they informed the New York City Police Department that two members of their staff failed to check in when expected and requested that they look for them. Salim was able to get to the police and ask for a complete news blackout and treat it as a State Department matter. The New York City police had so many cases on hand that they were happy to turn the matter over to the State Department. The State Department then turned the matter over to the FBI, and they were now on the case. Salim was worried that he would be caught with his hands in the cookie jar. Yaya and Ishy were not on an authorized trip. It was a secret and unapproved operation.

While Salim sat and worried, his mind went back to the time when Leo left for the United States. Salim, even though he had an invitation from Oxford University in England to continue his studies in genetics, decided to remain and continue his studies and work with Professor Dan Gill at the Hebrew University. Eventually, Salim got his Master's and his PhD. A few months after graduating and receiving his degree, the professor died. Salim was offered and accepted the professor's position in the university. The appointment included the professor's lab, and for Salim it also included the opportunity to renew his secret research work with the animals. Salim became one the youngest science professors in the university and probably in Israel, as well. He continued the experiments with the animals and continued to have some successes but mostly in similar species. He continued to change the contents of the gene soup but did not notice any improvements in the results. Then, almost by accident, Salim noticed that an offspring of a mouse he injected with the original soup, the one that Leo injected himself with, displayed some chromosome changes. Salim began testing the offspring and devised multiple tests for improved abilities of their senses. Since the animals obviously could not tell him about the test results, he had to figure it out. Test after test showed some promise but was not conclusive. Salim was always pushing for live tests on humans, but he did not want to endanger his position and the access he had to the lab.

A few years passed and eventually the university that paid his salary and supported the lab became unhappy with how Salim ran the lab he oversaw. Salim was very secretive with the research that he worked on. He obviously did not report on the research he did that was not approved, but he also did not report and share the information and results from his lab's approved genetic research. His department's head and the university's Ethics Department were not pleased. It was the Ethics Department role to determine that all research conducted in the university conformed to the university's standards and its commitment to safe and humane use of animals in the labs. Unbeknown to them, Salim spent more time and university resources on his secret research, money which he diverted from the university's directed genetic research. The powers that be in the university decided to close the lab down and offered Salim more classroom hours.

Salim was obsessed with genetic work. He invested years after Professor Gill's death pursuing the goals he laid out, and he was not about to give it up. He decided to find another benefactor that would allow him to do his research full time and quit the university. After a time and careful feelers, he was introduced to General Yousef Malik. He was the Military Attaché to the Jordanian Embassy in Tel Aviv. Salim found the General to be very interested in his genetic research, and the General thought that the Jordanian government would be interested in working with Salim. With the General's help, he was able to meet decision makers in the Jordanian government, who decided to support him. Salim thought that they did not really understand what his research was about exactly. Salim realized that in order to get them aboard he must give them a good reason to allow the Jordanian government to support him. His pitch was that his research results would allow them to come up with enhancements for their combat troops by making them super soldiers using the DNA manipulations that he had discovered, which he told them he had done for years in the Hebrew University.

There were a few Arab professors at that time but none in the Science Department other than Salim. He expected that his resume and the explanation of what his lab could achieve would excite them. He convinced them that if they funded his lab, it would yield spectacular results. He was sure they did not totally understand the science of what he was doing, but he knew that they would understand the goals and would be excited about the outcome and the opportunity, and he was right, they did. Jordan is a constitutional monarchy. That means that the hereditary king is the absolute monarch, but they have a prime minister that runs the government and a strong military, loyal to the king, and also a political power unto itself. General Malik was an able ally. He knew that the king and the military were concerned about a rising tide of discontent from minorities and disgruntled Palestinian refugees still living in squalor, in camps, in their midst. General Malik knew that the military was more than willing to take a chance on Salim's promises. He knew that they liked the possibility that they would have a process that would make their soldiers superior to those in the countries around them. The temptation was too hard to resist, and the cost seemed to be modest.

Jordan, which had an uneasy peace with Israel, gave him the funds to build a lab in Tel Aviv and a diplomatic cover job at their Embassy there. They also arranged for him to have access to their worldwide network of embassies. The money, while not a bottomless sum, still provided him with enough funds to establish a modern lab and continue his genetic research. Salim was able now to concentrate all his research efforts to come up with the right gene "soup." He was placing special efforts to follow the offspring of the animals he experimented with. He did not have to worry about reporting to anyone or treat animals humanely. He was in the wild wild west of research. He hired a protégé of General Malik, a former Jordanian military man named Raja who became his aide and provided security. He also recruited several other helpers including a scientist named Saud and two assistants, Yaya and Ishy, two unprincipled fellows who helped in the lab and ran errands, not all of them legal. He got them all diplomatic credentials so they could move easily in other countries and help bring back contraband.

Eventually, Salim concluded that the original "soup" was the best combination to get DNA mutations in the offspring, specifically in hearing, vision, taste, smell, and intelligence. The fact that the improvements were very minor frustrated him. He could not even conclude that they were from the "soup." Adding to his frustration, he did not detect any improvements in strength, agility, or speed, results he needed to please his Jordanian benefactors. He needed results in order to have the continued support from the General and his government. In addition, not all the offspring presented any mutations, so the results were not consistent.

Salim did not know when it began, but he started to think about Leo and the bet. He remembered Leo injecting himself with the gene "soup" and wondered if it had any effect on Leo or Leo's children. Did he or his children exhibit mutations that resulted in improvements in their vision, hearing, taste, smell, and intelligence? He was pretty sure that Leo was not affected, but Leo was the only human he knew who was injected with the gene "soup." Salim knew that Leo was now a professor in Cincinnati, but he did not know what he was doing exactly. He wondered what he was teaching and was curious if he had a lab. Salim was in contact with Leo sporadically, but Leo was secretive about what he was teaching or doing. Salim and Leo suffered a terrible tragedy some years ago. It was a tragedy that affected both of their families. Salim had a good relationship with Baruch and Meira after Leo left for the United States.

Leo's parents were in a shopping center with Martha when they met Adina and their son Bart. They chatted for a while and when they were all leaving the center, the sky opened up with a torrential rain. Baruch offered Adina and Bart a ride home, and she gratefully accepted. As they exited the shopping center with a blinding rain still coming down, Baruch lost control of the car and crashed into an embankment, killing all of them instantly. It was a major news event in Israel where such an accident, with five casualties, was big news and a devastating blow for both Salim and Leo.

Salim was in his office at his lab when he got the call. After the caller confirmed that it was him, he was told the terrible news. His shocked reaction could not have been extreme. He lost everything that meant anything to him. Aside from his research, his wife and son were all he cared about.

In the States, Leo got the news, as well. Salim did not know and could not know that Leo, a professor in Cincinnati, was secretly working with the CIA as a Middle East analyst and interpreter of documents. Leo got the news from his CIA handler. Leo and his sister Ruth flew in immediately. Leo and Ruth, who lost their parents and their sister, were in shock; but in spite of that, Leo realized that Salim losing his wife and child was incomprehensible. Leo felt that they suffered the loss together and tried to console Salim. Salim, on the other hand, as absurd and illogical as it was, did not feel the same. In Salim's culture, the biblical 'eye for an eye' was often taken literally by some. He blamed Leo for his loss. His reasoning was that Leo's parents killed his family; but since they were gone, Leo had to bear their guilt. He believed that his loss, and his wife and son souls, called for a response. In his now damaged mind, he swore to avenge their death.

As Salim returned to the problem he now faced and what he had to do about it, he realized that no one at the Jordanian Embassy in New York, except for General Malik, knew about his extracurricular work. They did not know that Ishy, Yaya, Saud, and Raja were his crew. He certainly did not want anyone at the Embassy to find out that fact. Yaya and Ishy were only tasked with a simple tailing job. They were supposed to find out where Rachel and her aunt and uncle were going.

Finding Rachel was a lucky break. One of Rachel's teachers at her school, a Muslim, told a friend at her mosque about a girl who lost her entire family after her dad and mom were killed and her siblings kidnapped. She thought it was tragic and innocently told her friend that the girl was now in her class and was mute, she couldn't speak. The friend, as friends often do, told the sad story to one of her friends in New York. It turned out that the New York friend worked at the Jordanian Embassy and told others, including one of Salim's crew, the story. Even though Salim had her three siblings, he was upset that they missed Rachel. He was anxious to find out if she had any special abilities. He still did not understand how they missed Rachel that first night. He was in the house; they went room to room making sure they did not miss anything. Now, all he asked Ishy to do was to keep an eye on her. He did not want her harmed or kidnapped. He knew that if something happened to Rachel now, the police and the FBI would connect the two. He was worried that maybe clues existed, and maybe they would increase their efforts to find the children. He knew that in the United States they spent more time, money, and energy looking for kidnap victims than for a murderer.

They had murder files open from the year of the flood. It took a lot of work to erase the evidence of their presence that night, and he wanted to play it safe. He was furious that now Ishy and Yaya were missing. They just disappeared, and the Embassy's security officers were completely baffled, as was he. There was bound to be a full investigation, worse he had no confidence that Yaya and Ishy would remain silent if they were in the hands of another party. Could they stay silent if they were questioned in harsh conditions? But who had them and why? Was it the police or was it Homeland Security? Did whoever grabbed them somehow find out about the weapons in the car and thought they were terrorists? He did not instruct them to take all this hardware. It seemed they did not know either, since they took Raja's car without his permission, and he foolishly had the hardware in the car. He could not afford to be exposed; he knew that he must make sure that no suspicion came his way. The Jordanians didn't trust Israeli Arabs too much. Getting this job with the Jordanians was very hard, and getting them to fund his research was always at risk. It was his fluent Hebrew and knowledge of Israel that got him this far. Now if they found out that Yaya and Ishy were involved in illegal activities, since they were under his supervision, it would be the end of the job and his dreams.

Salim knew that there were only two men other than Yaya and Ishy who could point the finger his way. He had to make sure that no one connected them all together. He went over in his mind carefully what could possibly point anyone in his, or their, direction if there was a careful investigation at the Embassy. The Jordanians were taught civil service by the British, who were the most thorough people on the face of this planet. He had to act and act fast. The kidnapping of the children was bad enough, but the murder of his friend and his wife was hard to forget. He knew that it was the only way he could be sure that the secret would be safe, but it was a high price to pay; and as hard and as greedy as he had gotten, there were still some small pangs of consciousness left in his cold heart. As his mind drifted again, he thought of Adina and his son Bart. He remembered the horrible tragedy that Leo's father caused. He lost his family, and his heart hardened again. There was some justice in Leo paying with his life and his family. He knew he would have to kill the children also when he was done with them, but his damaged brain did not comprehend the horrible deed he was contemplating. When his thoughts drifted back to today and the problems he faced, he thought, the children were well hidden for now; but he had to get them out of the country, and he had to do it soon. He could not afford to wait much longer.

CHAPTER 12

LEO'S DOUBLE LIFE

When Rachel, Aunt Ruthie, and Robin arrived at the police station, they had to wait a good hour for the desk sergeant to find the officer that made the arrangements with Aunt Ruthie so he could clear them in. Once that was done, they had to find a room for them to work in, and the property room people had to find the boxes from their house that contained her father's papers. They finally were led to and were seated in a small conference room that looked more like an interrogation room that they use to question suspects. After what seemed like hours, but was probably only a half hour, a policeman wheeled in a dolly stacked with a mountain of boxes. The boxes were all taped up with red tape marked GLICK. They looked at each other in surprise at the number of boxes that were wheeled in. They felt totally overwhelmed. Aunt Ruthie asked, "Where do we start?" She looked at Robin and Rachel with searching eyes.

Rachel kept her composure, though it was hard to see

her family's possessions wheeled in. She signed, "Let's find the boxes with the earliest papers first and then start the search by placing all the papers in sequence within the boxes."

Robin said, "Maybe we should discuss what we are looking for."

Aunt Ruthie responded, "If Leo did something to bring this about, we might see something that will give us a clue that we can then follow. We are looking for anything that could bring about such a horrible action."

They started going through the paper. The oldest dates went back to the Hebrew University. It appeared that Leo was a science major with a minor in languages. Ruthie related to them how adept Leo was in languages and how he picked them up so easily, "like you do, Rachel," she said. Rachel wondered, but only in her mind, whether her excellent hearing and sight came from him, as well. They split up the university papers and began to go through them, each with a notepad to write down any fact or events that might be important or relevant. Aunt Ruthie found a file that had a whole biography of a Professor Dan Gill. Evidently, Leo was very interested in him and his work. Rachel, who brought her computer with her, started up the laptop. She typed in the subject box, "Dan Gill," and a few Dan Gills came up. One of the posts was a Professor Dan Gill from Hebrew University. When she read his profile, it seemed he was teaching genetics. It mentioned studies of DNA. It did not give specifics of what exactly he taught or what specific research he did. She filed away the task of further research for later. She signed to the others, "If you find a transcript of dad's classes, see if he studied genetics or if there is any information about a class with Professor Dan Gill." There were other papers relating to courses he took but no other information concerning Dan Gill or genetics or DNA. There was no diary or any writing about his personal life. The box did not yield any other clues.

Rachel noted the absence of the information. She remembered from her readings of forensics and crime data that sometimes what was missing was just as important in crime solving as what was there. There was a box from the university in Cincinnati where he taught; but strangely, it had no official papers or credentials. The box mostly consisted of the type of information one would get when visiting the university. They found it peculiar and filed it away under open questions. There were several boxes that contained financial information, tax returns, and bank statements. Rachel felt they should go through credit card statements, but it seemed that other than year-end statements that gave totals by category, her father must have either done his credit card transactions on the internet or simply discarded the statements.

One statement that caught Robin's attention was an American Airlines reward miles statement. It had over a million miles in the account: 1,400,000, to be exact. Aunt Ruth was very surprised and angry that this fact was not revealed to her as the estate executor. Robin said, "These reward miles can be very valuable. Based on a rough calculation of one cent per mile, the award miles could be worth $14,000." Ruth was very upset that she did not know about the miles. It was a lost opportunity since they could have used these miles to travel to Cincinnati. Robin, who discovered the statement, wondered how and why Leo accumulated so many miles. it seemed like a lot for a university professor. She asked Rachel if she was aware of extensive travel by her dad, but she was not; and she agreed that this was something worth pursuing.

They had spent almost six hours in the police station. They were hungry, thirsty, and tired, and decided to call it a day and find a place to eat. They called the property room to come to pick up the cart and the boxes on it. They told the clerk they would be back tomorrow, and he promised to have the boxes for them when they arrived. They were pleased because it meant they would not have to wait too long. When they talked among themselves, the miles intrigued them. How and why did Leo accumulate so many miles? They decided to figure out a way to get to the bottom of it. Robin suggested that they visit the University of Cincinnati next and see if they had any of Leo's files. They could not believe that he only had brochures from the school.

They decided to go to a steakhouse, and Robin suggested that they go to The Precinct steakhouse. She thought that since they spent the whole day in the police station, going to The Precinct, a building that was actually once a police precinct and was now one of the best steakhouses in Cincinnati, was appropriate. Aunt Ruth and Rachel agreed. Robin looked it up on Google and read to them.

"This police station turned restaurant, The Precinct, located on the East Side of Cincinnati since 1981, is the oldest 'white table-cloth' restaurant of its kind in the city. The Romanesque-style building features rich warm wood interiors, red brick facade, and stained-glass windows. Signature steaks and succulent, fresh

seafood dominate the menu, while house-made ice cream and seasonal crafted cocktails add a touch of sweetness."

Rachel's mouth watered just listening to the Google search. She could not wait to get to the place and sink her teeth into a juicy steak.

After dinner, Robin dropped them off at the hotel and told them to be ready early in the morning when she came to pick them up. When they returned to the hotel, Aunt Ruth called the university. Once she found the right department, she explained who she was and wondered if the three of them could come by and look through any papers Leo might have left behind at the university. The Secretary at the Office for Faculty Affairs asked her to hold on; and after a few minutes another woman came to the phone. The woman identified herself as Ms. Williams, Director of Faculty Affairs, and asked who she was, what she was looking for, and why.

Aunt Ruth patiently told her, "My name is Ruth Mintz. I am Leo Glick's sister and the executor of his estate." She then went over the whole story and her request again. Ms. Williams asked her to hold on and after a lengthy time came back to the phone and told her that they had no records. She told Ruth that any records they had were picked up a long time ago. She also told her that any information about Leo was locked in the computer and no one at the university had access to it. A long back and forth ensued. Aunt Ruth insisted that as the executor of the estate she was entitled to know who took the records. She wanted to know why the university released them and asked if they had an inventory of what was taken. Ms. Williams was very understanding and patient but very firm. She had no answers. Furthermore, she did not know who would have more information.

Aunt Ruth hung up very frustrated and puzzled. She related the conversation to Rachel who found it very strange as well. Rachel wrote down two items to follow up on, the reward miles and the locked-up university records. Aunt Ruthie said that they did not even have the classes or other work records for Leo. Why would they not have that and why would that be locked up? Aunt Ruth found it very suspicious. Rachel thought about it and brought up to her aunt the two men with dark glasses she saw at the house and later in the limo on the highway. Why were they both at the house and on the highway? It all was very strange. They wondered if Leo could have been involved in some secret government project. Rachel signed "Is the whole thing some kind of a cover up?" They decided to sleep on it and go back to the police station in the morning and continue their search.

While they were sleeping, Joseph Brown and Adam Murphy were sitting in an office at the CIA building in Langley, Virginia. Earlier they received a call from Ms. Williams at the University of Cincinnati. She related to them, as she was instructed to do, that there was an inquiry about Leo Glick. She told them it was a phone call from Ruth Mintz. The day before, a sergeant at the police station alerted them that three women were going through the papers that they had from the Glick murders and kidnapping. This was a long-running case that they had just started unraveling with the arrest of the two Jordanian operatives, Yaya and Ishy, who claimed diplomatic immunity and gave them nothing else. The two, who they arrested in New York when they were watching Rachel Glick, were still not talking; but they were working on them, and they were hoping to break them soon. This latest development, the call from Ms. Williams, did not please them at all. They were the only ones who knew the danger that Rachel was in, and they were probably the only ones who knew that the kidnappers were after her. Leo was one of theirs, but it was a very delicate situation since the CIA was forbidden from working on U.S. soil, and they were doing just that.

The FBI were the lead investigators on the kidnapping, along with the Cincinnati police, and they were getting nowhere. The perpetrators and the children had vanished into thin air, and the arrest of the two Jordanians was the first break in the case. These orders came from high up. They had to guard Leo's cover, that he taught at the University of Cincinnati; and it was now in danger of unraveling. Joe and Adam realized that confronting the three ladies would be a bad idea. They were pretty sure, though it was an assumption, that Rachel was with Ruth; but they did not know who the third woman was. As far as they could tell, the women knew nothing. They were not aware that Rachel saw them the morning of the murders and kidnapping or when they nabbed Yaya and Ishy. How could they? But they had to contain the situation, as well. They decided to go to Cincinnati in the morning and follow the goings on from up close.

The next morning Rachel, Aunt Ruth, and Robin went back to the police station. They had to go through the same routine waiting to be cleared to go to their room and then waiting for the boxes to be brought up again; but the process, thankfully, was much quicker. They set aside the boxes that they had already examined and concentrated on the other boxes. As thoroughly as they searched, they did not find anything of interest. Rachel had another idea. She signed to Aunt Ruthie and to Robin that they should look for folders with hidden compartments or any hidden compartments in the boxes. She also suggested looking in the envelopes, maybe they would find something. One of the things Rachel found puzzling was that they did not find any pictures. She knew her dad had a camera and loved to take pictures, and yet they did not find any. After the resistance Aunt Ruth encountered at the University of Cincinnati, they began to suspect that something was not right. It was obvious that someone went through the boxes, as the investigators should have. It made sense that in an investigation of murder and kidnapping, everything had to be looked into. But it seemed to Rachel that papers, letters, and pictures that might reveal information were taken. They were assured that everything the police and the FBI had was given to them. Obviously, that was not the case.

They went back to each of the boxes, looked in the flaps, checked all the envelopes, and then one after one, in all of the flaps of the boxes. Finally, in one box they found a picture under the bottom flap. It looked like the box contained a lot more items that they could tell were missing. Perhaps this was where the pictures were taken from. It seemed this one photo, a very small picture that looked like it was taken with an old camera, must have found its way under the flap and was missed by whoever took the other pictures, at least that was their theory. The picture was of two youngsters perhaps six years old in a country setting. They seemed to be sticking their tongues out at each other in fun. Rachel took the picture and placed it in her pocket.

Aunt Ruthie said that she had some pictures from their childhood, and they could see if they would give them clues that might help.

It was another long day, and they decided that they had done all they could and found all they were going to find. They let the sergeant know that they were done and thanked him and the department for their courtesy. The sergeant, who must have been briefed on the purpose of their visit, said that he hoped it helped. They proceeded outside the door of the police station, and as they got to the street, Rachel froze. Some five hundred feet down the road she saw the limo. She did not see the two men with the sunglasses, but she was sure it was their limo, or at least a twin. She signed excitedly to Aunt Ruthie and Robin that the limo that she has told them about was there. The two, while still skeptical, agreed to walk over to the limo and check it out.

They walked slowly towards the limo; and as they got closer, they could see two men sitting in the front seats of the car. As they approached, the men got out, each from their side of the car, and came to the front to meet them. To the surprise of the women, they introduced themselves.

"I am Joseph Brown," said the man that got out of the driver side.

"And I am Adam Murphy," said the other.

We would like to invite you to come with us, if you care, so that we can share some information with you that I think you would like to have. With that, the man who introduced himself as Adam opened the rear door and invited them into the car. They looked at each other, trying to decide what to do. When Rachel slightly bent down and entered the car, Aunt Ruthie and Robin followed.

CHAPTER 13

THE LIMO

Joe and Adam drove the three women to their hotel downtown. The women were somehow not surprised that they knew where they were staying. It was inconvenient for Robin whose car was at the police station. They said they wanted to share some information and maybe get some information that they have. They asked if they could pick them up in the morning for a quick visit to their office. Adam said, "I think we have a mutual interest, but we cannot say any more right now."

Rachel was visibly excited and signed, "Yes, we will be ready."

When they looked at Aunt Ruth, obviously not understanding sign language, she told them, "She said yes, but we will talk it over. How can we let you know?"

Adam said, "We will be outside at 8:00 a.m, If you decide to trust us, just come out and join us." They then offered Robin a ride back to her car which she accepted. She told Aunt Ruth and Rachel she would see them in the morning.

When they got back to their suite, Aunt Ruthie thought they should talk it over, but Rachel signed that they were the ones that saved them from Yaya and Ishy. She told her again all she saw. Aunt Ruthie, who once had her doubts about that story, now believed her.

In the early morning Robin came over. They had breakfast at the Marriott and at 8:00 the women were ready and sitting in the lobby when Adam came in to see if they would go with them. The limo was outside with Joe at the wheel, and off they went. Joe drove towards the airport in Kentucky. As they crossed the river, Aunt Ruthie asked them where they were taking them. Adam told them that they were going for a short plane ride to Langley Virginia, but that they would be back for dinner. At the airport, they drove to a large building at the end of a long row of huge buildings. They drove into the building and saw a sleek, small jet plane parked inside. The limo stopped next to the plane and another man with a pilot's hat stood by the stairs leading up to the plane interior. Adam opened the door on the passenger side and Joe on the driver's side. They got out, and Joe invited them to go into the plane. They climbed up the steps. The plane was set up with comfortable seats along the sides, with an aisle in between, and the seats were all facing each other. Rachel could not contain her excitement and kept signing questions. When Aunt Ruthie related them to Joe and Adam, they just asked them to wait until they were at their destination.

As soon as they were seated, they were told to put on their seatbelts. Rachel noticed that all the seatbelts had a strap across the chest like the stewardess did. She thought, they want us to be safe. The plane started moving out of the building. It moved quickly to a runway and took off. It was not like the plane rides Rachel experienced before. The plane rose quickly. it felt like a rocket shooting straight up. As they neared their destination, they passed over Washington, DC; and they could see the mall, the Capital, and the White House. When they landed and the plane's door opened up, they saw an identical car as the limo waiting for them some twenty feet from the plane. They got into the car and it took off.

They arrived at a huge building in Langley and drove through some large metal barriers that opened as they approached. They parked near a set of doors and walked in. They were in a long corridor and they walked until they reached a set of elevators and got into one. They got off at a floor, they could not tell which, and walked into a similar nondescript hallway. They were led to a large room with a big table and very comfortable chairs. They imagined that it was a room where bigwigs met. Joe asked them if they would like anything to eat or drink, and Aunt Ruthie and Robin asked for coffee and perhaps a donut, and Rachel asked for juice and some fruit. Joe brought in some water bottles, coffee, and juice for Rachel and told them that they ordered donuts and fruit.

Adam and Joe sat down at the table and Adam said, "Let's get started, and let's begin sharing."

Aunt Ruthie began by asking, "How are you connected to the murders and kidnapping of my brother's family and why and how is the government involved?" They were shocked when Adam told them that Leo worked for the government. He told them that the University of Cincinnati professorship was a real job but also a cover, and Leo was an analyst for the

CIA, especially when it came to languages. His exceptional talent with languages was a very helpful skill for the CIA. It was all hush-hush at his insistence. It was an administrative type job, no danger to him or his family. Adam said he and Joe were his handlers and were very discreet and very accommodating. Joe explained that since his job was not very dangerous, at least as far as the CIA involvement was concerned, the murders and kidnapping were a complete shock to them. They were surprised and it presented them with a mystery they had been trying to solve. Leo was expected to call in every day; and when he did not check in, they were sent to check up on him. They came in after the police had already been on the scene for a while and decided to just hang back and get the information from them later. They were shocked that Leo and his wife were shot and the children kidnapped. They found it very strange and suspicious because they could not connect what happened to Leo and his family to the work he was doing for the government. They could not understand, for that matter, why the children would be a target. It was that last fact that confused them the most and made them suspect that something else was at play here.

At this point, they said they had some very shocking news for them and that they had to prepare themselves for it. They asked Ruth if she wanted to be told privately and then relate it to Rachel. She told them that it was Rachel who was in charge, and they could tell them all together.

Adam got right to it. He said in a somber voice, "Rachel, your father did not die. Your dad was gravely wounded and clinically dead until he was revived. He survived, but unfortunately, hasn't regained consciousness and is in a coma in a

CIA safe house." All three looked stunned. The news really did shock them. When Adam said he had shocking news, it was the last thing they expected.

All of a sudden, Rachel let out a loud scream. They all gasped. Rachel stopped like it was not her voice, like it was not her making the sound. After a moment of stunned silence, Aunt Ruthie and Robin both reacted at the same time. "YOU SCREAMED!" they both shouted at the same time, as if they rehearsed the reaction beforehand.

Rachel looked bewildered, "Did I make a sound?" she signed.

"You screamed," Aunt Ruth said, "try and say something."

Rachel turned to Adam and Joe and said in a loud voice, "WHAT ARE YOU SAYING? MY DAD IS ALIVE?" Joe and Adam just looked at them in puzzlement and asked what was going on. Rachel, Ruth, and Robin all began to cry. They got up, and got into a group hug. They hugged and sobbed and laughed.

Finally after several minutes, with Adam and Joe looking befuddled, Aunt Ruth told them that since that terrible night, Rachel could not speak or make any sound, her voice just went mute. She explained that it was determined that there were no physical reasons for it. It was psychological trauma that caused it. Considering what she had gone through, it was understandable. No previous treatments helped her, and the suddenness of the return of her voice surprised them, and of course gave them a cause to celebrate. The news that her dad was alive must have somehow got her voice back just as mysteriously.

Rachel, now obviously angry, asked "Why didn't you tell

us he was alive? It's my dad! And tell me where you have him, and when can I see him?"

Adam tried to calm her down as he explained that as they were taking him to the morgue in an ambulance, one of the EMTs checked his pulse. It was very weak, but he realized that the police just assumed that he was dead along with his wife and did not check him thoroughly. Adam had climbed into the ambulance as it was leaving and had witnessed the whole thing and immediately took control of Leo. They brought him back to a CIA safe house which was also a hospital they used and controlled. They arranged for Leo to be declared dead and to be buried with his wife. Obviously, his casket at the funeral was empty. Leo had been under watch with the best care but in a coma ever since. Adam told them that his vital signs were stable, and the doctors felt confident that he could recover. He was shot in the head and there was damage. They operated and removed a bullet. While it could take some time, people with similar trauma to the brain had survived and come out of the coma. He explained that since they did not know why he was shot and Rachel's mom killed, they decided to let the world think he was dead and the killers successful. They could not let anyone know, including Rachel and her aunt especially, since he was in a coma in a secret CIA installation. They apologized profusely and said that they planned to have them come and see him if he woke up from his coma, but they thought that until then it was best to keep it secret.

Joe said that they had Rachel, her aunt, and her uncle under constant surveillance and were not allowed to contact them and reveal the connection and thereby endanger them. Everything changed when they found out, through CIA informants and other means of getting information, that two Jordanians from the Embassy were sent after Rachel. They had the description of the two men, but they did not know their names. They also had a description of the car they were driving, the Mercedes. While the driver went into the terminal at the airport, they checked the car and saw that they had weapons and other trade craft that indicated that they were up to no good. They were tailing them when they became concerned on the highway, afraid they would attack Rachel's uncle's car while it was stopped under the overpass during the rainstorm, offering a cover for the attack. They decided to arrest them at that point and take them in for interrogation. That was how they wound up grabbing them on the highway. They were hoping that if, in fact, they were connected to the murders and kidnapping, they could find out how they were connected and why these crimes were committed. They were hoping to find out where the children were being kept now.

The two had a car-full of surveillance tools and weapons, enough to fight an army. So far, questioning them had been unsuccessful. While the CIA was not allowed to operate on U.S. grounds, there were exceptions, especially when it came to foreign operations on U.S. land, they explained. Finally, Adam said "We are quite sure that your mom and dad's attack had nothing to do with your dad's work for us, but we still don't know and cannot imagine the reason. We were hoping that perhaps we could learn more from you." Adam said that to show good faith they told them all they knew and all they did, and now it was their turn.

Aunt Ruthie and Rachel took it all in, especially that Leo was alive. Rachel did not know how she felt. She was happy, of course, that her dad was alive and upset that he was in a coma. She was also angry that the information had been withheld from her and her aunt. She left the room with her aunt, and Robin trailed behind. They were still in shock, to some degree, with all the revelations. After a few minutes, Rachel said emphatically, "I don't want to tell them anything until I see my dad." Aunt Ruth saw no reason to dispute her and agreed readily.

Robin said, "I think it is reasonable, given that it took a year to find out that your dad is alive. They allowed you to mourn and did not allow you the chance to see him."

They all shuffled back to the room and Rachel asked Adam and Joe, "When can I see my dad? I want to see my dad as soon as possible!" Joe said that he would take them to see Leo tomorrow morning.

Adam said that since it was already late afternoon, they would fly them back and drive them to their hotel and pick them up in the morning.

CHAPTER 14

LANGLEY

The flight back was uneventful, Rachel was getting used to this flying, enjoying the roominess and the refreshments that were provided. When they landed, they stepped into the limo that seemed much cleaner. It must have been serviced. She liked the smell of soap; it was better than the smell of gas and oil that accompanied the plane. Adam and Joe, ever the gentlemen, opened their doors when they got in and when they let them out at the hotel. They said their goodbyes and Robin left, as well, promising them to be there in the morning. Rachel and Aunt Ruthie were tired from the ordeal, and Aunt Ruthie was still getting used to Rachel talking. Both were still signing out of habit and often laughed as they realized that they were doing that. They ate at the hotel's restaurant and afterwards had little trouble falling asleep. They were spent, both physically and emotionally.

The next morning, they got ready, went downstairs, and met Robin. They were considering where to go for breakfast when Adam came in and said, "Let's go, we have breakfast for you on the plane."

Once again, they got into the limo and drove to the airport and the remote hangar and got on the plane. As soon as they sat and got belted in, the plane taxied to the runway and took off. It was not like the big heavy jet they came to Cincinnati on. It was almost like an amusement park ride. the plane just soared as soon as it was in the air almost straight up. Rachel loved the sensation and realized how preoccupied she was the day before since she did not notice the takeoff at all. When they were in the air and flying straight, a steward brought them trays of juice and water and coffee for Aunt Ruth and Robin. He took their orders like it was a restaurant. Rachel ordered pancakes and Aunt Ruth and Robin had eggs with potatoes and toast.

They landed in Virginia and, of course, another limo was waiting. They got in and drove for about a half hour to a building that looked like a cross between an office building and a factory. They parked near the entrance and walked in. As soon as they were in the door, Rachel knew they were in a hospital. She was able to take in all the smells typically associated with one. The antiseptic smell was very strong. Adam and Joe escorted them to a reception desk where they were given badges to wear and then they got on an elevator. Robin noticed that Adam had to enter a code into a pad before the elevator moved. They went to the third floor and entered a chamber-like room. They walked through a narrow passageway and saw an agent seated at a desk monitoring a big screen. Joe explained that they are walking on to a secure floor and that they were being scanned for hidden weapons. They passed through and went down the hallway passing a nurse's station and then went into a room with a hospital bed. They saw a man lying in the bed attached to humming and pinging machines.

Rachel rushed in and stood by the bed for a moment, not knowing what to do. Then she just bent down and hugged her father. He looked much thinner and had little color in his face, but he was breathing on his own and looked comfortable. He did not seem to be in an agitated state. He looked like he was in a deep sleep, and she guessed he was. After a while she moved away, and Aunt Ruth went over and hugged Leo, as well. A man walked in, obviously a doctor. He had a white coat and stethoscope hanging around his neck. He introduced himself, "I'm Doctor Sanchez. I have been taking care of Mr. Glick. His wound was quite severe and caused a lot of trauma. He has been healing, and we think that he has a chance of coming out of his coma. The body often shuts down with brain injuries to allow healing. Hearing your voices can help since we believe that even in a coma a patient has some awareness." Rachel did not want to leave, but Adam promised they would visit again soon and said it was time to leave and go back to their office. After some more hugs and kisses they left and rode with Adam and Joe to the CIA offices.

Once there, they went through the routine of checking in and then went back to the conference room they were in yesterday. After settling in, Joe asked Rachel to tell them what she remembered about the night of the murder and kidnapping. Aunt Ruth said, "I have to ask you guys a question. What is it with the limo? I always thought you guys travel in these big black SUVs?"

Adam chuckled. "We are spooks. We don't want to be

conspicuous, so we pretend we are limo drivers, sort of the unexpected."

Aunt Ruth said, "I guess that makes sense," then she turned to Rachel and told her to tell them all she knew from beginning to end and to not leave anything out. Rachel was, for the first time, able to tell what she knew from the terrible night without the need to sign.

She began by telling them how she woke up and heard faint noises. She could hear the screen door slide open, then the glass door sliding open, and then several separate footsteps, rubber soles on the tiled floors. She told them how she could hear them as they slowly crept up the stairs. She was in her brother Johnny's room; he was asleep next to her. She remembered that she was sleeping in his bed because he wanted company and she figured her bed would not be messed up and she wouldn't have to make it up in the morning. She told them that she realized that this fact saved her, and it was why she was not taken by the kidnappers, or worse, shot by them. She told them how she got out of the bed, how she moved slowly towards the bedroom door just as the first of the men got to the top of the stairs, how he was gesturing to the others, and it was how she figured out that he was the leader. The men were all up in the hallway, outside her parent's bedroom door, and they were wearing night vision glasses. At the time, she thought that these were funny goggles because she could always see in the dark, so she did not associate the two. Adam stopped her, "You can see in the dark?" he asked. She explained that she always could but thought that everyone could. She told them that she saw the man with the scar on his throat gesture to the others, and she figured he was the leader. She saw him gesture to himself and point to her parents' bedroom door and then to each door down the hall, and to one of the men. She told them that she was scared and sensed by then that it was trouble. When she saw the men approach her parents' room, she tried to scream but nothing came out. It was very weird and that was why she thought it was a dream. She knew she could talk, so the whole thing did not feel real to her. That was when her voice left her until yesterday.

She saw the leader of the group open her parents' door. He had a gun in his hand with a long barrel. She decided to hide in her brother's room, and then she heard a spitting sound like pfft... pfft... pfft... It was like someone spitting really loud. She knew now that was when he shot them. When one of the men came towards their room, she tried to scream again; but nothing came out. Her throat was para-lyzed. She told them that she naively thought they would not hurt anyone who was sleeping and so she hid where her mother stored the blankets at night. Just as the man came into the room, she dived into the chest and somehow was able to squeeze in behind the fluffy blanket so that she was covered. It was not a moment too soon. The man came in, and she heard one man tell the other in a very thick accent, from what sounded like her room down the hall, "Yaya, there is no one in here. Where is the girl?" She figured he was talking about her.

The other man, called Yaya, asked "Is the bed slept in?" The first man said that it was not, then the man called Yaya told him that she, meaning me, probably slept out if my bed was not slept in. I was happy to hear that, of course.

At this point, Adam interrupted her and asked her if she was sure the name was Yaya. She assured him that it was. Joe asked, "How do you remember all of this in such detail? You were twelve, in shock, scared, and it's almost a year later. How do you remember all these tiny details?"

Aunt Ruthie chimed in and explained, "Rachel has what her teachers and doctors said is a photographic memory, perfect recall. I also have to confess that up to recently, we did not believe Rachel's abilities."

Rachel leaned over and gave her Aunt a bear hug. "No one could be better to me than you and Uncle Joe," she gushed.

Adam asked Rachel to continue. Rachel continued her narrative. "So, this man called Yaya heard that my room was empty and the bed not slept in, so he said to that other man, 'Salim will not be happy.'"

Joe said, "Hold it! You said Salim?"

"Yes," Rachel reassured him, "it was Salim. This man Yaya," she continued her story, "told the other man to stop talking and called him stupid for talking. He said, 'Stop talking or you will wake up the boy. Let us do what we came here to do, and we will worry about the girl later.'" She told them that this was when she heard Karen scream, the kind of scream that was blocked by a hand over someone's mouth. The man called Yaya said that he wondered what was going on and said, "That Raja can never do anything quietly. Saud should be watching him."

At this point, Joe stopped her again and said, "So the names you remember are Salim, Yaya, Raja and Saud?"

Rachel replied, "Yes, and there is one more name," she said. "I heard rustling sounds, and then I heard the one called Yaya who I believed left the room, say 'Ishy, let's go check on Raja,' so Ishy was the fifth name I remember." She told them that she could hear them walk down the hall and could tell they went to Karen's room. She told them that she got out of the cubby and went over to the bed where Johnny was, but he was no longer there; and she remembered that she could not understand where he was. Did he hide or did they take him? If they took him, why? She told them she was very confused.

She continued that when she felt it was safe, she wanted to check on her mom and dad. A couple of the men were still in Karen's room, and Karen was still screaming with a hand over her mouth. She could hear one man say, "Hey, let's go," and she saw the men walking out carrying rolled up blankets with what looked like bodies in them. She assumed it was her brother and sisters. Rachel stopped and drank some of the water before she continued.

Her throat was raspy now. It felt strange after a year or so of not talking. The cool water felt good, and she let out a sigh. Then she continued, "Two men came back and took a couple of boxes from my dad's office and then they left. After the men went down the steps, I slipped into my parents' bedroom." She told them that she remembered that the clock said 3:30. She remembered also that she stepped on a metal cylinder, maybe a shell from a bullet, she guessed. She then discovered her mom and dad shot. She assumed they were dead, at least she thought so at the time and until yesterday, she added with a look of reproach. Finally, she concluded by telling them that she found out that her sisters were missing also.

Adam interrupted her and asked her what happened to that metal cylinder. She told him that it was in a little bag back at the hotel. "Why didn't you give it to the police?" he asked. She said at the time she did not think about it or realize that it was important. Later, her aunt must have washed her pajamas where she placed the item, and she took it out and placed it on the desk at the hotel they were in at the time. When she saw it again later, she placed it in a little bag that had contained earrings that her aunt bought her, and that was where it has been ever since. "The bag is always with me," she said. "It reminds me of the night and what I need to do."

Adam said, "This can be a clue."

Rachel responded, "I figured maybe it can be helpful. I will bring it tomorrow when you take us to see my dad again."

Adam asked Rachel to continue. She told Adam and Joe that she had wondered what her family did to these people to make them shoot her parents and kidnap her brother and sisters. She asked them if they had any clues. She said she had to find out who they were and where her brother and sisters were. She told them that she wondered, even now sometimes, if she was still dreaming. Joe asked her how she summoned the police if she could not talk, so Rachel told them how she got 911 to respond to her by banging the phone on the floor. She told them about Mike the Policeman who stupidly jumped to conclusions about her and set the tone for assuming she could not hear because she could not speak. They wound up speaking freely in front of her. She tried to tell them who did what and to whom, but they ignored her. When Rachel finished telling the full story, she was drained and visibly pale. Aunt Ruthie apologized to her for allowing her to tell the whole horrible story again, obviously adding to her trauma.

Robin, with tears streaming down her cheeks, just hugged Rachel.

Adam and Joe, who had been taking notes all along, were silent. When the three women finally calmed down, they began bombarding Rachel with questions. First, they checked on the names. Joe said, "So I gather you conclude that Salim was the leader," and Rachel said that he was. Joe continued, "and the others were, Yaya, Ishy, Saud and Raja."

Rachel agreed, "That's right."

Then Adam asked, "How about the accents? You said they spoke in a strange accent."

Rachel answered, "I think it was Arabic. I have heard that accent many times since that night. It fits with Arabic from Jordan."

After many more questions, many which just asked her to repeat what she told them already, Rachel told Adam and Joe about spotting Ishy on the plane to New York and then Yaya at the LaGuardia Airport luggage carousel. Later, watching them follow her uncle's car from the airport in their Mercedes. Eventually, seeing the men in the black limo, who she now knew was Adam and Joe, arrest them.

Adam and Joe were incredulous, "How did you recognize Yaya and Ishy? And how did you see us? It was raining so hard we could hardly see each other." Rachel explained that she saw Ishy on the plane, heard him speak, and recognized him initially from the voice. She tried to alert her Aunt Ruth but did not succeed. She then saw Yaya and recognized his voice, as well. She saw the two of them get into the black Mercedes and follow their red Eldorado four or five cars behind them. When Uncle Joe pulled off in the downpour, she saw the Mercedes pull over also a few cars back, and then she saw the limo which was following the Mercedes pull over behind them and arrest them. She saw them place the two in the limo and one of them got into the Mercedes and one in the limo and they drove away. It was all she could see, she said. Adam and Joe were dumbfounded. They could not believe she saw all that, but they knew it was all accurate. She explained that she had always had excellent hearing and vision. She also explained that she remembered seeing the same limo outside their home that horrible night.

"Well," Adam said, "it was us at the house, and we are still watching over your dad. But we want to continue having everyone think he is dead. It keeps him safe. We have Ishy and Yaya here. Now we have to decide what to do with them. We have not succeeded in breaking them. They claim they work for the Jordanian Embassy and have diplomatic immunity. We cannot hold them much longer. The State Department is already breathing down our necks."

Rachel said, "We have to get them to talk. They may know where my brother and sisters are."

"I know," Adam said, "it's been a long time since they were taken. While we don't know why, you now confirmed by whom. We think your brother and sisters are still in the country, but we are not sure. We also don't know if they are in harm's way. There has not been any ransom demand made, so we have no contact with the kidnappers."

"We have to find a way to get Yaya and Ishy to talk," Rachel said, "we need to find my sisters and brother."

CHAPTER 15

JOHNNY, KAREN, AND HEATHER

At the same time, in a windowless basement in the Bronx in New York in a house set back from the street, Saud and Raja were bent over a test tube containing a mixture of genetic materials that had been extracted from several different species. Saud knew that some samples came from animals that were protected; and if, in fact, it turned out that any of the soup concoctions he experimented with were an acceptable mixture, many of them would be killed to make large quantities. He had been playing the hard-working researcher for a long time and making no progress while being pushed to get results. Salim was now on a totally different level and it scared him. Working in this under-equipped and understaffed lab was not helpful to good science, but Salim insisted that they had to work here in New York, in the Bronx, in this old building. He was consumed with the idea that Leo's children held the key to the success of transplanting the genes of special abilities of animals to humans. No amount of proof that they had no special abilities got him to believe that they were just normal kids.

Saud was still playing the nightmare of the kidnapping over and over in his mind. He was aware that Leo had worked with Salim but did not know the whole story. He had been a researcher in Jordan when Salim recruited him. He was a scientist but not at the same level as Salim. No one would suspect that he was doing the work he was doing, given his background. He knew it was dangerous, but it became more dangerous for him when Salim forced him to go along on the mission to get blood samples from the Glick children. He did not know that they would kill Leo and his wife, nor did he know that they would kidnap the children. The plan, he was told, was to use ether to make them sleep and then take blood samples and maybe other samples from all of them. Salim told him that he wanted to make sure that the extraction would be done properly. He doubted it and figured that Salim just wanted him along so that his hands would be dirty, as well, and then Salim would have something on him and be better able to control him. He knew Leo was a professor at the university, but he sensed that there was a lot more to the story and that there were lots of missing pieces.

Later, when the children were in the Bronx, he found out that Salim's plan was to test the children's senses and draw blood and genetic materials from them to see if they had any mutations that gave them improved senses from the soup that was injected into Leo. Salim did not share the fact that Leo injected himself with the soup until they went to the Glick house. The new research now introduced with Leo's children was an unwelcome complication, and Saud was very uneasy with that. Raja hanging around, he thought, was Salim's way to keep an eye on him. He felt that Salim did not trust him.

Johnny, Karen, and Heather were all in a room in the basement apartment. The room was soundproof and roomy. It had three beds, a desk, and a small bathroom with a commode, a sink, and a shower. They had a treadmill that Salim said they would need to use for exercise, and they had a bureau of sorts in which they had a change of clothes that he prepared. Saud felt a pang of guilt now remembering how they shot Leo and his wife; and then he, Yaya, and Ishy carried the children out and packed them into the back of the van and took off. Raja stayed behind to clean up and cover their tracks. Raja was ex-military, a former high-ranking officer who Salim recruited. He provided security and muscle. They were in the van almost twelve hours, driving from Cincinnati to New York. They had to be careful not to speed or draw attention in any way, given their passengers in the back of the van. They made several short stops for bathroom breaks and to get some food. The children were passed out. They had given them an injection of a mild sedative, enough to keep them sleeping. After what seemed like an eternity, they arrived in the Bronx at their hideaway. The children were taken out of the van and were carried into the basement and into the room that was prepared for them and was going to be their room for the foreseeable future.

When they woke up, the children were disoriented and confused. They had no idea where they were and why they did not wake up in their own beds. They hugged each other and then Karen went to the door and began to pound on it. "HELLO!, HELLO!" she yelled.

A voice with a distinct accent said, "Please stop making so much noise. Be quiet and soon we will talk to you."

Karen walked back to Johnny, who was sobbing, "Where is mommy? Where is mommy?" She hugged him and tried to quiet him down.

She said to Heather, "I don't know what is going on yet, but we will find out soon. The man on the other side of the door said he will talk to us soon." She did not let them know that she knew they were kidnapped. She remembered the man who came into her room; and when she screamed, he put his hands over her mouth. She tried to bite him without much success and continued to try and scream, and then she smelled something very medicinal, and that was the last she remembered until now. She came back from a deep sleep disoriented, not having any idea what was going on. She thought, *Where is Rachel, and what happened to her parents?* She knew that for the sake of her brother and sister she had to keep it together; but she was scared and worried, especially for Johnny.

At some point later, they heard a noise at the door and then the door opened, and a man walked in with a tray of food and bottles of water. He placed it all on the table that was against one of the walls, and said, "Now eat and drink and someone will come back a little later and explain everything to you. You are safe here, and no one will harm you." He turned around, closed the door behind him, and left the room. They heard the click of the door locking.

Sometime later the man came back and picked up the trays and empty bottles. He brought towels and told them to go to bed because it was late and they would explain everything in the morning. They showered, slipped their pajamas back on as they still had them from the night before, and went to sleep. In the morning, the man came back. He told them his name was Saud. He brought them cereal, milk, and juice and then left. Later he came back with clothes for all of them and told them that someone would come and talk to them soon.

It was several hours later when they heard the lock click again and then another man walked in. He introduced himself, "Hello, children. I am Salim." He asked them to sit down, and he began his explanation. "Children, I was a friend of your father's for many, many years. We went to school together in Israel and became very close. We recently found out that your father and your whole family were in grave danger. It seems that a group of terrorists found out that we worked on research together, and they wanted to kidnap the three of you and try and get your father to cooperate with them. Tragically, your father reacted very aggressively to protect you, and the kidnappers killed your mom and your dad. As they heard the news, all three began to wail. Salim tried to quiet them, but they would not be consoled. Finally, he told them that he would come back later to finish telling them what happened.

When he got up to leave, Karen, who was still sobbing and holding Johnny who was wailing, said, "Where is Rachel and why are we here?"

Salim, now invited to continue, sat down again, and continued his story. "When we found out about the attack," Salim said, "we rushed to your house. We were too late to save your father and mother, but we were able to save you. Unfortunately, the killers got away and we are afraid they are still looking for us so we drove all night from your home to this hideaway and we will stay here for a while until it is safe. It's very dangerous and we all have to be very careful. For a while, you have to stay here. We will take care of you and soon we will be able to move you to a safer place." Karen asked again where Rachel was; and Salim, with the first honest words he spoke, said "I really do not know, but I will try and find out. She was not with the killers when we rescued you. We went back to the house and searched, but she was not at the house. We have friends out there looking for her, and we will let you know as soon as we find out."

The children were exhausted and depressed, and they just collapsed together in a heap on one of the beds. Over the next weeks and months, the children fell into a routine of studying, exercising and tests. On a few occasions, the man who they now knew was Raja, came in and drew blood from the children, using some excuse, like checking them for the flu or some other medical reason. They developed various tests for the children under the guise of having to submit them to allow homeschooling, and they monitored their physical exercising and their abilities when it came to their senses. Saud and Salim wanted to find out if the children had any special abilities, but they did not find anything exceptional about the children.

Truth be told, Salim was getting very nervous. He still had not heard from Yaya and Ishy, and no one had any idea where they might be. Yaya, especially, had been a very dependable ally. Raja and Saud were getting nervous, as well. Their work with the children had not produced any results and did not seem to give any indication that results were imminent. It had been almost a year. Salim did not accept personal responsibility for the lack of success. After all, Professor Gill failed and he was their teacher and leader in the research; but he was frustrated and had become very impatient lately and had accused Saud of spinning his wheels. It was like someone was pushing him for results and he had to push everyone else.

Salim felt he had a decision to make: what to do with the children and what to do about Saud and Raja. The children were actually a dead end, and he wanted to bring about an end to this disaster. He wanted to get back to his lab in Tel Aviv and close loose ends in the United States. He was very worried about Yaya and Ishy. The only one he trusted was Raja. He knew how to take orders and how to execute them, he thought. While Saud was a good researcher, he had to go. He knew too much, and he felt he could not trust him.

CHAPTER 16

THE PLAN

Back in Langley, Adam, Joe, Rachel, Robin, and Aunt Ruth were still trying to come up with a plan when Aunt Ruthie suggested they take a break for lunch. Adam called down and ordered sandwiches and drinks, and they took bathroom breaks.

While they were in the bathroom, Rachel heard Adam speak to someone. She assumed it was Joe, but of course she could not see who it was. "Do you believe what the little girl went through?"

The other person, who she now was sure was Joe, said, "Yes, but I am amazed that she remembers everything so clearly; and tell me, how could she see us arresting Yaya and Ishy through the rain and at that kind of distance?"

She turned to Aunt Ruthie and Robin who were getting ready to leave. "Did you hear that?"

"Hear what?" they both responded.

"Adam and Joe talking," she said. They both did not hear

a thing and said so. They wanted to know what she heard and how she heard it.

"I have an idea," she said. "Let's go back and I will share it with you." They went back to the conference room. The staff at the CIA must be very efficient, they thought, because a tray of sandwiches and various sodas and water bottles awaited them. They ate their lunch and chatted about their trip and how long they planned to stay. Robin told them that her week off was at an end soon, and she had to get back in the next day or two. Aunt Ruthie said that they would stay as long as they needed to, and Rachel nodded enthusiastically. Ruth and Robin thought that Rachel was not yet used to talking and still used nonverbal communications. Aunt Ruthie said she was still shocked, amazed, and ecstatic that Rachel could talk; but she told them that she never understood why she couldn't speak, given that all the experts found nothing wrong with her voice box physically. And now, she did not understand how Rachel's speech returned instantly the way it did. "I guess the mind is amazing, and we still know so little about it and what it can and cannot do," she said.

Rachel decided that this was a good opening for her idea. Addressing Adam she said, "Did you tell Joe "Do you believe what the little girl went through?" and Joe did you respond, "Yes, but I am amazed that she remembers everything so clearly, and how could she see us arresting Yaya and Ishy through the rain, and at that kind of distance?"

Both Adam and Joe looked at each other with open mouths. They both said almost at the same time, "How did you do that, did you plant listening devices on us?"

Rachel chuckled and said, "No, of course not. I have no

way of planting devices on anyone, but I always had excellent hearing and great vision. Until that terrible night, I didn't think it was unusual. I thought everyone has the same eyesight and hearing." She related to them that when her dad explained to her what she now knows were night vision goggles, to see in the dark, she did not understand what people needed them for as she saw pretty clearly in the dark. But after that night when she saw the men wear goggles and realized that she could see without them, she then realized that she could hear sounds and voices that no one believed she could hear. She started suspecting that she had abilities beyond others and became aware of other abilities and talents she possessed. They wanted to know about her other abilities; but she wanted to get on with her idea, which was an unorthodox method of getting information.

Rachel thought that if they could freak out Yaya and Ishy and get them to talk to each other, maybe they could get them to reveal information. They listened intently as Rachel presented them with her idea. She began, "My idea is that you place each of them, Ishy and Yaya, in separate cells in complete darkness. I will enter their cell in a way that they will feel a physical presence near them, but not see me. Then I will repeat the things they said to each other during their murderous attack. After hopefully freaking them out, I will leave. The lights will come back, and they will each see an empty room. Afterwards, we will place them in the same cell and listen to them talk to each other. I believe that one of them will start with the telling of his experience and then the other will relate a similar one. I expect that they will try and figure out what is going on; and I expect by acknowledging that what they heard is what they said, they incriminate themselves." She told them that she was sure they would, it was human nature. She continued, "Once they have said enough, then you can leverage that to squeeze information from them. Hopefully, when they realize that they gave up the operation, they will turn on the organizer of the murders, and you can then find them and find my brother and sisters' whereabouts."

When she was done, Aunt Ruth was the first one to react. "There is no way you can do that, Rachel," she said. Robin, Adam, and Joe all agreed. Aunt Ruthie continued, "Why would you even think about getting anywhere near these killers?"

Rachel said, "This is the only way I can think of getting them to talk. They will not respond to traditional methods of interrogation. They probably got trained to resist interrogators or lie and tell them stuff they want to hear to misdirect them. My way is better. The only risk I see is that it will not work, and that is a low risk compared to having nothing, I think."

Adam was the first to change his mind. "You know, it's crazy, but it just might work. Let us assess the risks." Since Yaya and Ishy were being held under national security provisions, they were not accorded attorneys or any other rights at this point, including diplomatic immunity. They still had plenty of time before they transferred them to the State Department or the FBI. After all, they had them for almost six months. Adam explained that he had to run the idea up the chain of command since it entailed some risk, expenses, and getting a minor involved. He also added that, if approved, he had to make the proper preparations for the ruse, including listening devices, infrared cameras, and a way to darken the area so it was completely dark. Adam suggested that the women go visit Leo. After that, he would fly them back to Cincinnati and then come back tomorrow, by which time he would have an answer for the next step. A young man came by and said he would take them to see Leo and they left with him.

General Shaffer was in his office when the two agents called and asked to see him immediately. After bringing the General up to date, they brought up the problems they had getting information from the two prisoners and presented Rachel's plan. When the General stopped laughing, he said, "Are you kidding me?" Adam and Joe then told him about Rachel's hearing and other enhanced senses. They explained that they did not even understand them themselves, but they did experience them. When they explained why they thought this would work, the General stopped laughing and became thoughtful. "What are the risks?" he asked. They reviewed together how the ruse would be played and the potential things that could go wrong. Rachel could be seen or exposed in some way. When Yaya and Ishy were together, they might not talk about their experience or, if they did, say nothing useful. They concluded that other than exposing Rachel to some danger which they could control by standing by with a stun gun, they felt the only danger besides that was that the plan would not work. At the end, the General approved the plan, the equipment, and whatever they had to do to make it work.

In the meantime, Rachel, Aunt Ruth, and Robin were driven to the hospital pretending to be an office building to visit Leo. They went through the same routine they did the prior day, and Rachel and Aunt Ruthie spent some quality time with Leo while Robin waited outside in a waiting room. They talked to him like he was awake, and Rachel held his hand. Her sensitive hands literally felt his heartbeat through his fingers. She felt so close to him and thought how ironic it was that now that she found her voice, she found that her father did not have his. After an hour or so they said their goodbyes and were taken to the airport for the flight home.

When they got back to the hotel, Robin told them that while she would love to meet them in the evening, she could not spend the next day with them. They went together to have dinner in the hotel and then said their good nights.

The next morning Aunt Ruthie and Rachel went to IHOP for breakfast. It was Johnny's favorite, and so it was now Rachel's favorite. She decided to really go hog wild and ordered the waffle with the happy face. It was lots of chocolate and whipped cream. After breakfast, Joe came to pick them up. They were getting used to this routine of chauffeured cars, fancy jets, and breakfast served while flying. When they landed, they were driven to the CIA offices and shown into the same conference room. Adam came in and gave them the good news that their boss approved the plan. Adam told them that he and they had preparations to do.

Rachel asked Adam if they could be taken shopping for some special clothing she thought she would need. While he was making a call to arrange for it, she told Aunt Ruthie, "We need to get some appropriate clothes. I think I need an all-black outfit."

Aunt Ruthie responded, "I am all in for shopping, you don't have to say it twice," and so they all left and were driven to their favorite store, Macy's.

Adam and Joe set to work. They chose two interrogation

rooms and placed infrared cameras and sensitive microphones in them. They made sure that the doors were flush with the floor, so in case accidentally some light came on outside the room, it would not filter into it. Ishy and Yaya were kept in separate cells. They had to decide if they should move them together tonight or wait until tomorrow night. Since the plan was Rachel's, they called her and asked her opinion. She reminded them that whichever cell or room the two of them wound up in, it had to have all the electronic setups, as well. She thought if they could get it done right away, then moving them together tonight would be better. Get them used to talking together and, who knows, maybe they would give some information before we even executed this plan.

When Rachel and Aunt Ruth got back, she was dressed in her new black clothes. She also had with her a black head covering called a Hijaz, usually worn by religious Muslim women. Adam and Joe looked approvingly at her. They both agreed she did a good job shopping. It seemed that everything was ready to go in the morning. Joe took them to see Leo, then flew them back to the hotel and promised to see them bright and early tomorrow.

YAYA AND ISHY

Yaya was proud of himself. He has steadfastly denied everything and kept insisting he was just out for a drive in an Embassy car and did not know about any equipment in the trunk. He kept claiming diplomatic immunity and requested to speak to his Embassy and to a lawyer. He had not seen Ishy since he was taken out of his car and handcuffed, blindfolded, and brought somewhere in a plane. He was kept in a room, isolated, and interrogated intermittently. He worried about what Ishy was saying and what Salim was thinking and doing. He hoped that Salim knew of his arrest and was working to get him out. Ishy, likewise, had been resisting all efforts to get information out of him. He also claimed diplomatic immunity and refused to answer questions. When asked about the weapons and other military equipment in the car, he too said he was just a passenger in a car going for a ride and knew nothing about what was or was not in the car.

In the evening after he received and finished his dinner,

Ishy was brought to a cell which was larger than the one he was in before. It had two beds and sitting on one of them was Yaya. He was so happy to see him and rushed over to give him a hug. "How have you been?" he asked him.

Yaya said "I have been fine. They have treated me pretty good except for the interrogations and the food. How about you?"

"Except for the fact that I have not seen you until now, I am okay, pretty much like you."

Yaya asked him, "What did you tell them?"

"Just like we agreed, we were just on a ride to nowhere. I claimed diplomatic immunity and kept asking to be released and to see a lawyer."

"Me, too, but they just ignored me. They said they found weapons and other stuff in the car and that we were arrested under the terrorism act or something."

Ishy asked, "Do you know where we are or who arrested us?" Yaya said he did not know but did not think it was the police since he knows they were flown somewhere. He thought maybe it was the FBI. "So far they have not used any torture or any kind of other means to get information from us," Ishy said, "I wonder if they are ready to let us go?"

Yaya responded, "I am surprised that after all this time that we have been missing, the Embassy has not been successful in finding out where we are and getting us released. We are part of the Embassy."

Ishy said, "They must be concerned. We just disappeared. Don't you think they would be making an effort?"

After a while and some more idle chat, they laid down on their new beds and went to sleep. Adam and Joe listened to their conversation. Other than the comment showing they rehearsed their answers beforehand, nothing of substance was heard.

Rachel and Aunt Ruthie were up early the next morning. Rachel got dressed in her black outfit and they went down to the lobby to meet Joe who met them and drove them to the plane for the flight to Virginia. They had breakfast on the plane and after landing, they were driven to the CIA office. Rachel asked about her dad, and Joe told her there was no change. He promised her that they could see him later. They all gathered in the conference room, and Adam started running through the preparations and the plans.

Joe started the conversation by questioning whether they should do the ruse with both. "I thought about the sequence of the plan. I assumed that we would take both of them from their joint room and place them into separate interrogation rooms. We will begin interrogating them and at some point the lights will go out and they will basically have the same experience. Then let's assume the lights will come back on, the interrogation will continue, and they will be led back to their room. At this point, they will compare notes and find out that they had the same experience right after they were placed in the same room after months. If they have a small bit of sense, they will figure out it was some kind of ruse. I think we should do it only with one of them. Do the blackout with both but the visit from Rachel with only one of them. That way when they discuss it, one will be a skeptic. I think it will get more of a reaction and less suspicion."

Rachel said, "That was not my plan, but it makes sense." She asked Adam and Aunt Ruth what they thought.

Aunt Ruth said, "I am a bad one to ask, I do not like this

whole plan. I think it's too dangerous. It's risky and there is no guarantee it will work."

Adam was deep in thought. He was pulling on his chin and finally said, "Joe, you never cease to amaze me. I think you make a lot of sense, too. I think Yaya is the more senior of the two so we can try it on him and play the whole thing as a regular interrogation, interrupted by a blackout. We can use the fact that we put them together because we hoped that the goodwill we displayed would make them more cooperative. For Ishy, it will be an interrogation interrupted for the same amount of time as Yaya. For Yaya, it will be an adventure. We hope that it will blow his mind."

Joe said, "Then we are in agreement. We will try the plan only on Yaya." Rachel and Adam nodded their agreement.

"So, let's review," Adam said. "We take both Yaya and Ishy into separate interrogation rooms. Joe, you will take Ishy and I will take Yaya. After about 15 minutes, the lights will go out. Joe, you and I will walk out and lock the doors. Before my door is closed, Rachel will sneak in and the infrared cameras will begin recording. Rachel will do her thing and when she is done, we will wait a few minutes. I will open the door, she will leave, and I will say that the lights should come on any second, and presto, the lights will come back. Both Joe and I will continue with the interrogation, finishing with Ishy first, so he will be in the room when Yaya comes back. I do not expect that either will cooperate. We will reconvene in the IT room to see if the plan worked. How does that sound?" Both Joe and Rachel agreed that it was a go and Aunt Ruthie just shook her head.

Two agents were sent to get Yaya and Ishy and escort them to the interrogation rooms. Adam and Joe moved to the rooms to begin the interrogation. Rachel waited outside the room where Yaya was being questioned and waited for the lights to go out and the door to open. Adam and Joe went through the same routine as they rehearsed. They began by telling the two that they hoped they appreciated being together again. They then began their respective interrogations, more or less asking the same questions they had asked many times before. They asked each of them why they were in a car full of weapons. If they were not their weapons, whose were they? How long did they work at the Embassy? What were their duties? They assured them that if they cooperated, more accommodations would be made, and they might even go free. About ten minutes into the session, the lights went out as planned. It was total darkness. Yaya and Ishy were in handcuffs that were connected to the table. That was important to make sure that they could not get up and move around. Joe and Adam followed the script and told them to stay put while they went to see what was going on. They both groped their way out and Rachel sneaked into Yaya's interrogation room.

Rachel made an effort to control her breathing and get adjusted to the tiny amount of light, too little to be seen by normal vision but enough for her to see all that she needed. She began to repeat word for word Yaya's conversation at the house that terrible night. "Yaya, I went to the girl's room. I looked in there, but the bed was not slept in," she half whispered.

"Who is there?" Yaya yelled.

Rachel said, "So it's obvious if her bed was not slept in, the girl either is in one of the other rooms or maybe slept out at a friend or relative."

Yaya yelled again, "Who is there? Who are you?"

Adam opened the door. It was pitch dark in the hallway, as well, "What is all the yelling about?" he asked. Yaya said that someone was in the room. Adam said, "You must be hallucinating, there is no one here but us. Sit tight, they are working on the lights. We should have them shortly." With that, he slammed the door.

Rachel said in that same half whisper voice, "Salim will not be happy. Stop talking, stupid, and stop talking before we wake the boy up! Let's do what we came here to do and get out. We will worry about the girl later."

Yaya let out an audible gasp, "Who is that?" he yelled, "who is here?" I must be having a breakdown, he thought.

Rachel continued repeating their conversation with her perfect recall, "Why is the girl screaming? I wonder what happened over there. That Raja can never do anything quietly. Saud should be watching him. Ishy, let's go check on Raja."

Yaya was holding his ears, "NO, NO!" he shouted. "Stop it, stop it."

Adam thought that it was enough, and he executed the last of the steps. He opened the door and told Yaya, "Calm down, are you afraid of the dark? The lights should be on any minute." With that, Rachel snuck out and magically, the lights came back on.

Yaya blinked his eyes with the harsh light back on. He looked pale and absolutely scared. "You look terrible," Adam said as he sat down opposite Yaya.

Yaya looked back blankly at him and said "Why don't you just let us go? We have done nothing." He did not sound very convincing.

"Why don't you tell me how long you have been in the United States." Adam continued with the interrogation as if there was no pause. Yaya told him and so it went on for another fifteen minutes with Adam getting nowhere, and Yaya just looking haggard. Finally, Adam figured that Joe was done with Ishy and said, "Okay, for now we will stop but we will continue tomorrow."

Yaya said, "You are wasting your time."

Adam replied, "I have all the time in the world."

Adam left the room and one of the agents came in, undid Yaya's cuffs, and took him back to his and Ishy's room. The group met in the IT room and Adam asked Joe how his interrogation went. Joe said it was the same result as always. They all gathered around the screens showing the room Yaya and Ishy were in and waited to see what happened.

Yaya threw himself on the bed and buried his head under the pillow. Ishy looked concerned, "Are you okay? What happened? Did you crack?"

Yaya sprang up like a spring and said angrily, "No, I did not crack; but I did have a very strange experience."

"What happened?" Ishy asked.

"Well," Yaya started, "the lights went out in the room."

"I know," Ishy interrupted, "the lights went out in my room, too."

Yaya looked up and asked, "Did you hear anything while the lights were out?"

"No. What do you mean?"

"While the lights were out, I heard a voice. It was right in front of me. It was as close to me as you are."

"A voice?" Ishy asked, "what did the voice say?"

"It repeated every word that we spoke to each other when we were at the Glick house."

"BINGO!" Adam yelled and raised his hand to give a high five to Rachel, then to Joe. He turned to Aunt Ruthie and stopped, but she raised her hand and he slapped hers, as well. Ruth and Rachel hugged.

Joe shushed them. "Okay, stop celebrating. Let's hear the rest." They turned back to the screens and watched the two Jordanians discuss Yaya's strange experience.

Yaya said, "I have not thought of that night in such detail ever. If you stuck a gun in my eye, I would not remember all the details. How did that voice know all that stuff?"

"You think it was a ghost? Well, we did kill two people, maybe they are back to haunt you."

"I did not kill anyone," Yaya said angrily. "It was Salim. I only carried that little boy out and took some records and a computer."

Ishy said. "I know. I am sorry, but if it is someone from the other side, why you?"

"I don't know, but I am so tired of being here, watching what I say, and where is Salim or the Embassy? I think they forgot us."

"Did you hear enough?" Rachel asked.

"Yes," Adam and Joe said almost at the same time.

Rachel said emphatically, "So now let us get them to talk and find out where Johnny, Karen, and Heather are."

Adam replied, "Let them talk some more. We are taping everything and will continue the interrogations tomorrow. We got a confession to murder and to being an accomplice to murder. They are going away for a long time, and we certainly have a lot to bargain with. Rachel, your plan worked like a charm, and we are in debt to you. Now it's our turn to deliver. Why don't you go visit your dad? Then we will take you back and we will see you tomorrow."

Rachel and Aunt Ruthie were taken to see Leo. Rachel sat next to him, held his hand, and talked quietly to him. "Hi, daddy. It's me, Rachel. Aunt Ruthie is here, too." As soon as she began to talk, she felt a changed sensation in his hand. "Daddy, if you can hear me, squeeze my hand." He did. It was a pressure that no other human would have felt, but she did. "Oh my goodness, you can hear me," she said louder now and felt the squeeze again. "Daddy, I know you are in there and getting better. Please come back to us as soon as you can." This time she felt the pressure twice. "Daddy, if you understand my question, squeeze once for no and twice for yes." She wanted to make sure that yes was more difficult. Aunt Ruthie was sitting just outside the room; and when Rachel's voice became louder, she looked in and heard Rachel talking to her dad. A nurse walked by and heard some of her remarks and walked in as well. Rachel said, "Daddy, do you know who shot you?" She felt her hand squeezed twice. She became more animated. "Was it Salim?" She felt her hand lightly squeezed twice. "Did you hear him shoot mommy?" She felt the pressure twice. "Did you realize Salim shot you?" Again, the two faint squeezes. "Is that when you fell to the floor?" Again, the two squeezes. She could feel the pressure diminishing, and she intuitively knew that he went deeper under. He probably got tired from the effort. She thought it was best to stop. She had all he could possibly give her right now.

After she gave her dad a hug and a kiss and told him she loved him, she motioned Ruth out the door. Aunt Ruthie went into the room, gave her brother a kiss on his forehead, and they left for the airport and back to the hotel. Rachel had one more confirmation that Salim was the killer. She could not wait for the interrogation tomorrow. On the plane, they called Robin and invited her to dinner.

Aunt Ruth and Rachel reached the hotel and went to their room. Rachel was still dressed in the all-black outfit, which now became a relic, changed, and then went downstairs to meet Robin. Robin was ecstatic that the plan worked. They realized that the interrogation would be challenging, Rachel said, "We have to get them to tell us where Johnny, Karen, and Heather are." They talked about various other stuff and then said their goodbyes. Robin left, and Ruth and Rachel went upstairs, showered, and collapsed onto their beds.

CHAPTER 18

THE CONFESSION

The next morning Joe was waiting for them downstairs, and the day's routine began. They were driven to the airport. Once on the plane they got a good breakfast and after landing were then driven to the CIA offices. The routine changed, though. Instead of the conference room, they were escorted to the IT room. In the IT room, a large TV screen was on a wall with the view of a table and chairs in a room. It was one of the interrogation rooms from yesterday. After some ten minutes, Yaya and Ishy were escorted in and were seated facing the cameras. Soon, Joe and Adam came into the IT room. They greeted Rachel and Aunt Ruthie and told them that they were getting ready for the big reveal. Rachel said she had some more news for them. She told them about her experience with her dad. By now, Adam and Joe were ready to believe everything. She explained that she asked her dad questions; and in response to her questions, her dad squeezed her hand as she asked him to, once for no and twice for yes. Rachel said, "The most important thing is that he is in there and hears everything. The second most important is that he confirmed to me that Salim is the one that shot him and my mom."

Adam said, "That is good to hear. We can use that information when we confront those two killers."

"We will both be in the room grilling them. If they don't crack now they never will, so here it goes," said Joe.

Adam and Joe left for the interrogation room while Rachel and Aunt Ruthie sat back, watched them enter the room, and greet Yaya and Ishy tersely. Yaya and Ishy looked both puzzled and arrogant at the same time. Yaya actually spoke first, "When are you going to honor our diplomatic immunity and let us go? It's been six months and my Embassy must be going nuts with you holding us illegally."

Adam responded, "You must be really important because we have not heard from your Embassy or from anyone else. You two are not going anywhere until you begin to cooperate."

Yaya said, "You can wait a long time for that, it's not going to happen because ..."

Joe interrupted him in mid sentence and addressed both of them. "Before the two of you embarrass yourselves, let me give you some important information that might influence what you say. We have new evidence that will put you away for the rest of your lives, so stop making statements that will do you no good and just make it worse for you. You notice that you are both together now. That is because the games are over, and we know everything. You were part of a group of terrorists that attacked the Glick family. You killed Mrs. Glick and wounded Mr. Glick. You kidnapped three of their children and tried to kill or kidnap their fourth child. Your crew included two other terrorists named Raja and Saud and were led by a terrorist named Salim. How am I doing so far?"

Rachel was amazed at the visible change in Yaya and Ishy's facial color and expression. They both turned white as the color drained from their faces, and they lost the arrogant look they came into the room with. Adam chimed in now, "Let me tell you that Salim was identified as the terrorist that shot Mr. Glick and his wife. Mr. Glick identified him by name. He must know him; and Salim, in turn, obviously must know Leo Glick. Now it's up to you. We know you were there, so you are accused terrorists. As terrorists who have murdered or aided in murder, you will be sent to Guantanamo, tried, and probably sentenced to death. Your Embassy probably knows you are goners because we have heard nothing from them. You two are on your own, hanging out to dry, no one wants you, or are coming for you."

Both Adam and Joe just sat back and looked at Yaya and Ishy who looked sick. Finally, Ishy said, "We did not kill anyone. We don't know what you are talking about."

Yaya added, "You don't know anything, and you don't have anything."

Adam said very calmly, "You know, Yaya, sometimes our own conscience begins to get to us. Maybe you are a nicer guy than you think. It seems that something inside you made you have some visions, am I right?"

"What are you talking about?" Yaya said, looking even more worried and confused. Adam raised his hand and made a circle in the air, a sign that signaled let's go. A sound came on the speakers above. Yaya's voice came over clear as a bell.

"I have not thought of that night in such detail ever. If you stuck a gun in my eye, I would not remember all the details. How did that voice know all that stuff? You think it was a ghost?"

Ishy's voice came on, "Well, we did kill two people. Maybe they are back to haunt you."

"I did not kill anyone," Yaya's voice said angrily, "it was Salim. I only carried that little boy out and took some records and a computer".

Ishy's voice was heard again. "I know you did not kill anyone. I am sorry I said that, but if the voice is someone from the other side, why you?"

Yaya's voice said, "I do not know, but I am so tired of being here, watching what I say, and where is Salim or the Embassy? I think they forgot us."

Adam raised his hand again with a closed fist, and the sound went dead. "So," Joe said sarcastically, "you talk to ghosts but not to us? You obviously want to come clean. I can tell both of you that kidnapping can result in as harsh a sentence as murder, and being in the same house, on the same operation, taking orders from the chief terrorist, is not a very good place to be. You are best off cooperating with us, helping us find and rescue the children, and find Salim. You should pray to your God, and the voice that you heard, that the children have not been harmed. This is your chance to get some leniency, but it has to yield results." Joe added, "We are serious. We will send you to Guantanamo and no one will ever see or hear from you again."

Yaya took a long breath and said, "Okay!, Okay! But you have to tell me, was that a trick? How did you do that? How did you get the information? And how did you do all that stuff when it was dark?"

Joe said, with the sincerest expression, Rachel thought, "It was your guilty conscience, Yaya. You are obviously not totally lost. Maybe there is some humanity left in you. So let us help you both. Tell us everything you know. Don't leave anything out and start from the beginning."

Yaya, still with obvious fear and maybe with still some doubt said, "What are you going to do for us?"

Joe said, "We can recommend that you get lower sentences and then be allowed to serve your time in your country. We have done that for others, and you can be sent back to Jordan to serve your prison time if you want."

Adam said, "But first, we have to find the children and Salim, so start talking."

Yaya turned to Ishy and said, "I think we should take a chance on these guys. Salim will assume they cracked us anyway, so I think we are in big trouble either way."

Ishy, who had been quiet all this time said, "I am no martyr. I never liked taking the children. That was not the plan, and I certainly was not for the killings. That was all Salim."

"Okay," Yaya said, "we will tell you all we know." He began, "We have been working with Salim for quite a few years in a lab in Tel Aviv, Israel. Salim was a professor at the Hebrew University when he left to start his own laboratory working for the Jordanian government. I do not know why he left. I heard that at the lab he was doing research into genetic mutations. Why he was doing that or what he was researching was above our pay grade. He used exotic animals for his research; and on occasion, we had to go and get an animal and bring it back to the lab. From a lot of the yelling and arguing, I know things did not always go his way. Saud was one of the scientists that worked with him; and Raja, who is ex-military with the Jordanian army, was mainly in charge of security and sometimes went with us to get animals."

Adam asked, "Which animals and do you know why?"

Ishy chimed in, "We went to Africa and brought back a cheetah once. Another time we brought back a desert fox and once an eagle. We heard he was doing experiments with animals. I know there were a lot of mice and rats, and they used to train them to run in mazes all the time."

Adam asked, "When and why did you come to the States?"

Yaya said, "It was about 16 or 18 months ago. We were all registered as working for the Jordanian Embassy under Salim. He was officially the science advisor to the Consulate. Salim and Saud started a lab in New York. We were doing odd jobs for the Embassy but in reality worked secretly for Salim. About a year ago, we were told to go to Cincinnati, find the Glick family, and keep Salim informed of their whereabouts. We found his house and tracked Leo Glick to his job at the university. We reported back to Salim and Saud about the location of the house where the family was and where Leo worked. Then we were all called to a meeting where Salim told us that we had a mission. We were supposed to sneak into the Glick house and use ether to knock everyone out. Then Saud was going to get blood samples from everybody. We were supposed to clean up and leave."

Adam asked," Do you know why they wanted their blood samples?"

Ishy replied, "No idea, it probably had something to do with the experiments and research Salim did. I know that he knew this Glick from Israel, but that was a long time ago."

Joe asked, "Did you know that Leo Glick was CIA?"

At that, both Yaya and Ishy looked at each other and then at Joe and Adam, "Is that why we are here? Are you CIA?"

"So," Joe said," from your reaction, I would gather that you did not know. Do you think that Leo Glick, being with the CIA, had something to do with the mission?"

Ishy said, "No, we never knew that. We also do not know why Salim killed the parents. We are happy to hear that Mr. Glick is alive and are sorry his wife was killed. We were surprised when he had us take the children. We don't know if that was the plan or just happened at the last minute. We were told that Glick had four children, but one of the children was not there. When Salim told us to take the children, we were told to take her, also. Salim was very upset that she was not there; but her bed was not slept in, so we figured that maybe she slept at a friend's house. I know that Saud was very upset that Salim killed the parents and was kidnapping the kids. The only one that seemed not to be upset was Raja."

"So what happened next?" Adam urged them to continue.

Yaya said, "We loaded the kids into a van that came with us. Saud gave the kids an injection for them to sleep, I guess; and we drove to New York."

Joe asked, "Where exactly in New York?"

Ishy said, "It was a building in the Bronx. I don't know

the address. We took them into the building and into a basement apartment. There was a room ready for them. It was in the same building as the lab they set up. The place has a dining room and bedrooms. It seemed like a big apartment."

"How big a building was it?" Adam wanted to know.

Ishy said, "It was maybe four or five stories high. It looked more like a factory than an apartment building. I did not see anyone else there. We were only there for a few days. Afterwards, we went back to work at the Embassy until I was sent to Cincinnati."

Joe asked, "Why were you sent back to Cincinnati?"

"It seems that a teacher that Salim knew, or someone who knew someone who knew Salim, any way, they told him that a girl in that school lost her parents and her brother and sisters were kidnapped. So he was convinced that she was the girl that we missed at the house, and he sent me to find her. I went to the school with a picture Salim gave me of the girl. Her name is Rachel. I saw her leaving the school, and I followed her to where she was staying and reported back to Salim. He told me to keep an eye on her. I hung around the school and made friends with one of the teachers. She told me that Rachel was moving. I made some more inquiries and found out that she was moving to New York. When I told Salim, he seemed to be really happy. He told me to keep following her, and when she went to the airport to get on the same plane and that Yaya would meet me at the airport. He wanted us to follow her and let him know where they were headed. I followed them to the airport, but when I tried to get on they had no more seats, so I had to buy a ticket in first class."

"Tough break," Adam quipped.

"I guess," Ishy continued, "it was a nice break for a change. We all usually have to fly coach when we travel, while Salim is always in first class. When we were getting off and I was standing in the aisle waiting, I saw Rachel. She was in the first row and standing on the seat. She looked right at me. It was weird. It was like she recognized me which of course was impossible because she never saw me before."

In the IT room, Rachel giggled and looked at her Aunt Ruthie, who just smiled. They were riveted to the screen as Yaya and Ishy were telling their story. Rachel thought it was all true because so far it fit everything she knew.

Ishy continued, "When I got off, Yaya was waiting for me. A man that I assume was Rachel's uncle came to get them. They got into a red Cadillac and we followed. We were not going to harm them, I swear. We were just following them to find out where they are going."

Yaya let out an audible sigh and looked at Ishy. Joe asked Yaya, "Does that fit with everything you know?" Yaya nodded his head. "So tell me," Joe asked, "why the hardware in the car?"

Yaya looked a little embarrassed. He said, "I really don't know. I was late leaving for the airport and I went to the Embassy's basement and just grabbed a car. I had no idea what was in the trunk. I did not even open the trunk. I have no idea why the stuff was in there. The keys were in the Mercedes that Raja usually used, so I thought since Salim was sending us, he wouldn't mind."

Ishy said, "I swear to Allah we did not know what Salim was up to, and we did not know that Mr. Glick was CIA. You have to believe us."

"Well," Adam said, "I wish Yaya saw ghosts six months ago. You would have been much better off and so would we. Now, for your sake, I hope the children are safe and we find them where you said you took them." Adam pressed a button on his side of the table, and a young man came in all business. He undid the handcuffs that bound Yaya and Ishy to the table, cuffed their hands behind their backs, and led them out. Adam and Joe returned to the IT room where Rachel and Aunt Ruth waited for them.

CHAPTER 19

THE BRONX

"So, it's the Bronx," Adam said. "Sounds to me like they gave us the whole story. How did it sound to you, Rachel?"

Rachel agreed, "It fits with all the information I know. I don't care if Ishy and Yaya knew or did not know that Salim was going to kill my parents. I guess there is a big difference between drugging and taking blood samples and killing and kidnapping; but they were a party to both, and they certainly did not report it. They continued to be part of it."

"I agree," Joe said. "The only reason they confessed is thanks to your abilities and your brilliant use of them. You cracked the case, Rachel; and now we will go get your brother and sisters and put Salim where he belongs."

"So what is our plan?" Rachel said very seriously.

Joe chuckled, "Your plan is for you and your wonderful Aunt Ruth to visit your dad and say goodbye to him for now. We will take you back to Cincinnati and you will go back home. We will keep you posted as to what happens."

Adam added, "We have to contact the FBI and the New York City Police. We cannot just burst into New York. As you might know, we are not allowed to operate on U.S. grounds. We have already taken some risks with Yaya and Ishy."

Rachel looked at both of them intently. "You need Yaya and Ishy to show you where the building is since you don't have an address. You need me to locate my brother and sisters, I can hear them from a distance you can't; and I can be of help in other ways, as well. You can't just shove me aside now. Without me, you would be nowhere."

Adam looked at Joe and they both smiled at her ferocity. Adam said, "Look, we have to talk to the FBI and the New York City Police. If we tell them that we want to bring along a 13-year-old girl to confront terrorists who have killed and kidnapped, well, you can imagine how that would go."

Rachel did not relent. "You can have me in your car and bring me out if you need me. You do not have to tell them. We will go to New York with you, and we will stay out of the way. Johnny, Heather, and Karen will need us. Who knows what kind of shape they will be in and what lies they have been told."

"She makes a lot of sense," Joe said.

"Wait a minute," Aunt Ruthie all of a sudden jumped in. "Rachel, I will not allow you to go on a raid like this. This is not your decision. I cannot have you in danger like that, and I certainly don't want to be part of a dangerous police action."

Rachel said, "Auntie Ruthie, we have to go. We have to find them. We have to help. This is my Bat Mitzvah present, remember?"

"Well, I am sure that these nice gentlemen will not allow it," Aunt Ruth said with a tone of finality.

"Well, actually," Adam said, "it's not a terrible idea as long as we have the two of you together and off site in case we need you for the children. I think it might be useful, but let me work this out with the FBI and the New York City Police. You go visit Leo and go back to your hotel in Cincinnati. We will pick you up or send for you as soon as we are ready to go. We probably will not leave until the morning."

Rachel and Aunt Ruth took that familiar route to see Leo and spend some time with him. Rachel told him how they were doing, the confession, and that they were planning to go after Salim. Rachel did not tell him that her mom, his wife April, had died, or that her siblings were kidnapped. She felt that very slight pressure every now and then and especially when she told him how much she loved him and that he had to get well and come back to them. She told him that they had to leave now but would be back soon. After the visit, they were driven to the airport and flown back to Cincinnati. They went to the hotel and packed their stuff, ready for the flight back to New York.

Back at the Jordanian Embassy, Salim was busy shredding any piece of paper that had his name or anything to do with him or his work. Salim was a guest at the Embassy, and he did not report to anyone. He wanted nothing to remain from his stay there. When he left, he wanted it to be like he had never come and was never there. He called Raja to his office and told him that he heard from his friend who knew one of Rachel's former teachers in Cincinnati, the one who was close to the teacher in the school that Rachel attended before she left for New York. That woman helped them find her some six months ago, "Well, she is helping us again, and we have to act and act fast. She found out that another teacher by the name of Robin took a week off to spend with Rachel and her Aunt who came to Cincinnati. She found out that Leo is alive. I have no details about him. She said that the girl who was mute found out that her dad was alive and began to talk again."

Raja asked, "How did he survive? You shot him in the head. Is this why they are in Cincinnati? Maybe they came to visit him and that teacher Robin. I can locate her and get her to tell us why they came here and maybe where Leo is."

Salim was obviously agitated. "I have a very bad feeling about the whole operation here. It has been almost a year since we grabbed the Glick kids, and we are no closer with our research. So far, the kids have been no help. Yaya and Ishy have been gone for six months now, and no one knows where they are."

Raja reminded him, "You know my car had all that hardware in the trunk. They probably think they are terrorists. I am sure they will not be connected to us. Yaya and Ishy will not talk. I am sure of that, too."

Salim said, "I am not so sure, and I am not going to take a chance. They know where the lab is and where the kids are. If Leo is alive, they know that I am involved. It is time to put this all to bed. That building has to go up in a cloud of smoke. I booked a flight back to Israel. We have to take care of Saud and the kids and then get out of here."

Raja looked a little surprised. "You want to kill Saud?" he asked with an edge to his voice.

"You have a problem with it?" Salim said in a threatening voice. He added, "I do not trust Saud. He is too soft. If they get him alive, he will fold like a deck of cards. We have to get out clean before anyone is onto us. We do not want to be caught here, that I am sure."

Raja asked, "So why not just leave?"

"Because it will follow us wherever we go. It's been a year, and no one has bothered us, at least until now. I figure the police, the FBI, or whoever have no idea who we are, what we did or are doing. It's time to pull up the stakes and get out of town."

Raja saw that there was no point in arguing. "Okay," and left to gather his things in the Embassy and destroy what he did not want to take with him.

When Aunt Ruthie's phone rang, she was happy to see that it was Robin. She brought her up to date and told her they were leaving in the morning. Robin was a little agitated. She said she wanted to see them. Aunt Ruthie told her to come right over. When Robin came in, she looked upset. Rachel and Aunt Ruthie sensed that she was troubled but thought maybe she was upset that they were leaving. Robin finally sat down and told them that she was upset to find out that a fellow teacher was talking to a friend in New York about a conversation they had about Rachel. The teacher asked her why she took off for a week; and not thinking it mattered, she told her that she wanted to spend the week with Rachel, her former student, who came to Cincinnati. Robin, on the verge of tears, told them, "The teacher asked me if that was the girl who lost her parents and could not talk, and I foolishly became too comfortable with her. I was so happy that Rachel found her voice when she heard her dad was alive, and I thought this teacher had no connection to you both. I told her that Rachel's voice came back when she found out that her dad was alive. I immediately regretted it and felt so stupid. She left the room and I followed her to ask her to please keep it confidential. When I saw her on the phone, I got closer and heard her tell someone on the other end of the phone all that I told her. I generally don't like to assume or be accusatory, but that teacher is Muslim, and I thought maybe that was how the killers found Rachel when she left Cincinnati. So I rushed here right away.

Rachel said, "I think that's bad. Let me call Joe.

She dialed his number, and he got on the phone right away, "Is everything okay?" he asked, sounding worried. Rachel had never used this number before.

"No, it's not!" Rachel said, getting right to the point. "We think that Salim has an informant in the school that I went to here in Cincinnati, where Robin teaches." Rachel related to him the conversation Robin had with another teacher, revealing to her that Rachel's dad was alive, and that Rachel had been visiting with him here in Cincinnati. She got the impression that this woman, who is a Muslim, communicated this information to Salim either directly or through someone else. Joe told her he would call her right back and hung up the phone.

A short time later, Joe called back. He sounded rushed, "We are on the way to get you. A local colleague of ours will be outside your hotel in one hour. Pack your bags and go downstairs. He will take you to the airport. We are all heading to New York tonight. Adam is already on the way with Yaya and Ishy. The operation in New York has to be carried out by the New York City Police and the FBI. They are very good when it comes to dealing with terrorists. We can only watch and consult. We will follow as soon as I can get to you. It will take about 90 minutes so we should be off again as soon as we land.

Robin, who was still apologizing constantly, helped them pack up all their belongings; and they rushed down with their suitcases. A good-looking young man was in the lobby waiting for them. Aunt Ruthie went to the hotel's desk and checked out, and they hugged and said goodbye to Robin. They went off with the young man to the airport; and when they arrived, they drove to the hangar they always took off from. After some 20 minutes, a plane taxied into the hangar, a ground crew rushed over and climbed all over the plane, brought over a hose to fuel the plane, and another young woman opened the car's trunk and took their suitcases and loaded them on the plane. They were invited to get on the plane, and Joe was on the phone, waving them in. They settled into the seats that, by now, they were used to from their daily journeys and waited for Joe to get off the phone. Several minutes later they were taxiing outside to a runway that must have been cleared for them. Unlike the slow inching forward they were used to with commercial flights and even at times with the flights back and forth to D.C., the plane never slowed up until it took off. It climbed so quickly that Rachel thought she was on an amusement park ride again.

Joe finally got off the phone. He turned to them and said, "We had the Jordanian Embassy under surveillance and identified Salim as he was leaving. We are assuming that a man that was with him is Raja. They were followed and headed to the Bronx. Once we heard from you that he might know that your father is alive, we figured he might assume, therefore, that we have a lot more knowledge to flip

Yaya and or Ishy, and it would spring him to action. Who knows what he might be up to. We also found out that he booked a flight to Israel, so we know that he plans to leave. The New York Police and the FBI are already in the Bronx and so is Adam. Yaya confirmed that the building they followed Salim to is the building that they dropped off the Glick children. They are getting ready to go in because they are concerned. They are afraid that Salim and Raja are up to no good. The officers that followed Salim and Raja reported that on the way to the Bronx, they stopped at a gas station and filled up a few cans with gasoline. They are very concerned. They have the New York Fire Department standing by, as well."

Rachel and Aunt Ruthie listened with alarm. Rachel asked, "Do they know if the children are there?" Joe said they didn't know but assumed that they were.

It seems like it was hours, but it was just under one hour when they felt the plane start the descent. Once again, it felt as if they were on an amusement park ride. It was a quick dive, and when they felt the plane straighten out, it was already landing. There was a big "Welcome to New York and LaGuardia Airport" sign. They pulled up to a gate, and the plane's door opened. It was also the stairway, and they went down the stairs and into a car that materialized next to the plane. Somehow their luggage appeared, the trunk opened, and they placed the luggage into it. They barely got a chance to buckle in when the car took off like a rocket. They shot out of the airport onto a highway. The car had one of those flashing light devices that the driver placed on the roof of the car on his side. Rachel saw with relief that the cars were getting out of the way as they sped along. They drove onto a long bridge, the sign read "Throgs Neck Bridge," and a few minutes later they were in the Bronx.

Rachel was looking out the window when she saw in the distance, off and below the highway, lights flashing. There must have been ten or fifteen vans and police cars. They got off at the exit and soon joined the swarm of cars. Rachel wanted to bolt out, but Joe stopped her. "Let me find Adam and find out what is going on. You stay here. I will be right back." He left, and Rachel got out and stood next to the car straining her ears and her eyes. It was dark now, but she could still make out dozens of men in various attire, some in police uniforms, some in fatigues, and some in plain clothes. They had gear all over them.

A few minutes went by and Joe came back with Adam. "We got the kids," Adam said, "I will take you to them in a minute. We are told that Salim and Raja got there first and killed the man that was there. We assume that it was Saud. They had set up the gasoline cans with timers that the police and fire fighters disabled just in time. I think they were going to make it look like Saud set the building on fire and shot himself. The children were in a room, and we had to convince them that we were there to rescue them. They must have known that they were in danger and had barricaded the room they were in. We must have gotten there just in time because Salim and Raja had taken off, and the timers were stopped with seconds to go. Thanks to God we got to them when we did. The New York Police and the FBI are looking for Salim and Raja. We hope to hear an update soon."

Adam took a breath and Rachel said, "Where are the kids?" Adam told her that they were being checked out by the doctors in the ambulance and that he would take her to them.

Adam led them under yellow tape that was now strung all over and then led them around the vans and cars, all still flashing their lights. It was an eerie scene. Rachel saw a big ambulance before they were even close and heard her Johnny, Karen, and Heather before she saw them. When they got to the ambulance, Adam opened the back door and Rachel jumped in and before a word transpired, they all jumped in each other's arms and began to cry. It was a cry of relief and happiness; it was a release that was long in coming for all of them. Adam, Joe, and Aunt Ruthie were all outside watching the reunion; and Ruth was crying, too, for that matter, Adam and Joe's eyes were moist, as well. Rachel knew that a lot of heartache was still in front of them, but right now she was just happy that her brother and sisters were safe. After they disengaged, she stepped outside and gave her aunt a big hug. Then she went over to Joe and Adam and gave them each a big hug. She could not believe that it had been a week since Aunt Ruthie and she left for Cincinnati to find them.

WEST HEMPSTEAD

A few hours after the event in the Bronx, a big black limo pulled up in front of Aunt Ruth and Uncle Joe's house in West Hempstead. Johnny, Karen, and Heather were escorted into the house. Aunt Ruth and Rachel rushed over to greet them and hugged them. Johnny clung to Rachel. They all finally sat down on the couch in the living room with their arms around each other. They just needed to feel that it was real, that they were really free and that they were with people they love. Aunt Ruth, as a therapist, knew that it would take a good deal of time for them to heal.

Uncle Joe came in and suggested that he order a pizza. It was amazing that all three of them cringed visibly. Karen said, "We are sick of pizza. That is what they fed us most of the time."

Aunt Ruth jumped to the rescue. "What would you three want?"

Heather said, "I want anything but pizza."

Karen said, "Also, no hamburgers from McDonald or Wendy's."

And Johnny said, "Can I have pancakes?"

Aunt Ruth, Uncle Joe, and Rachel looked at each other, smiling. "You know what kids? It's almost breakfast time, so how about if I make everyone my pancakes with chocolate chips and whipped cream?" Their eyes lit up. They obviously had not had it in a year.

Johnny wanted to know where mommy and daddy were. He said, "The men told us that bad men killed them and you too, Rachel, but you are here. Where are they?"

Rachel said, "These men you were with were the bad men. Daddy is very sick, and mommy is in heaven. How about we all talk about it tomorrow. We want to know what they did to you and how you spent your time." Rachel could not get over at how close she came to losing all of them. If Robin had not called, they would not have been on time and Salim would have murdered them. She shivered thinking about it.

It was very late, and they were all exhausted. The kids just wanted to sleep. They washed up and went to bed. Johnny crawled next to Rachel and was out like a light. Rachel had a harder time falling asleep. Her mind reviewed the last 24 hours and was thinking already about how to get Salim.

Salim and Raja, after they picked up the gasoline, had rushed to the Bronx. When they arrived at the building, they went to the basement. Saud, who must have already retired, came out. When he saw Salim and Raja, he smiled, and his eyes went to the gasoline cans. "What are these for?" he asked.

Salim told him, "We are going to light the place up. They are onto us, and we need to get away!"

"What about the children?" he asked.

Raja said, "We are going to light them up, too."

Saud screamed, "You cannot do that, they are children. They haven't done anything to you."

"You are right," Raja said, "we cannot light them up. You will."

Saud's anger rose. "I certainly will not!" With that, and without another word, Raja shot him in the head. Saud fell with a look of surprise and a final breath. Salim took the gun from Raja, wiped the gun clean with a handkerchief, and placed the gun in Saud's hand.

Then Salim told Raja, "Let's quickly set the timers and get out of here." Raja set the timers and attached them to the cans of gasoline. He placed one next to Saud, one by the children's door, and one at the entrance. They set the timers for ten minutes and got out by the front door. They locked the door and as they were about to get into their car, they saw the vans and the police cars descending on the building. They backed the car quickly around the corner and rushed towards New Jersey.

Raja said, "You are going in the wrong direction. JFK Airport is the other way."

Salim said, "That was just a ruse in case they come after us, which I am sure now that they are. I arranged for a private plane to take us."

They arrived at the Teterboro Airport in New Jersey and drove to the private hangar area, and the hangar with the waiting plane. They flashed their Jordanian Embassy identity papers and unloaded several bags from the car's trunk which included papers and the weapons, all with diplomatic seals. They asked one of the mechanics to park the car in the airport public parking garage later and entered the waiting plane. A few minutes later the plane left the hangar and took off for the flight to Jordan. Once on the plane, Salim opened the bags and took out several boxes and the weapons. "When we are over the water, we will get rid of this stuff," he told Raja. A few hours later over the ocean he directed the pilot to descend so that they could open a door and discard the weapons and the offending records. When the plane was at an altitude where it was safe to open the door, they got it open. Salim stepped to the door and tossed out all the hardware he had, then he told Raja to toss out the boxes, and finally told Raja to toss out his gun. As Raja stood in the open door to toss out the gun, Salim shoved him out. Raja, with a look of surprise, reached out his arms in a vain attempt to reach and hold onto something; but of course there was nothing to grasp. With a scream that quickly faded, he fell. Salim started screaming himself, as if he just witnessed a terrible accident. He rushed to the cockpit to tell the pilots about the horrible tragedy that just befell his friend.

Back at the CIA Hospital, another miracle was occurring. Leo opened his eyes. It was early in the morning and a nurse had gone in to check on him. She was shocked to see that his eyes were open and following her. She was so surprised that all she could say was "Good morning."

Leo looked at her and said, "Good morning. Where am I?"

"You are in a hospital. You were shot and were in a coma."

"What hospital is this, and where are my wife and my children?" At that, the nurse shook off her stupor, regained her composure, and went to get the doctor.

After the children and Ruth left, Adam and Joe went to speak to Yaya and Ishy. They were shocked when they were told that Salim and Raja killed Saud and set up gasoline bombs to kill the kids. They both thought that Salim had lost it. Before they were turned over to the New York City Police with a recommendation for consideration for the information they provided, they gave Adam and Joe the address of Salim's lab in Tel Aviv. Joe called his contacts in the Israeli Mossad, the equivalent and counterpart of the CIA, so that they could follow up and arrest Salim when he arrived. They knew that he had booked a flight to Tel Aviv. They still had another mystery; the booking was only for Salim. They figured that either Salim killed Raja also, since he seemed to get rid of his crew one by one, or something else was afoot.

The hospital had orders to notify Adam immediately if anything changed in Leo's condition. He did not expect him to wake up. When Adam got a call later in the morning, he was still groggy from lack of sleep from the night before. He had to ask several times, "He's awake?" Adam called Joe and they immediately took off for the hospital. Joe could not believe that Leo was awake.

Rachel woke up in the afternoon since they all passed out after breakfast. She turned to her side and was surprised that Johnny was lying next to her. The prior night's event came flooding back, and she was overcome with emotion. She hugged her sleeping brother and went to look for her sisters. As she went into the hall, her Aunt Ruthie greeted her with her finger to her lips pointing to the living room where her sisters were sprawled out on the sofa sleeping soundly. Aunt Ruthie motioned her into the kitchen and offered her a cup of coffee. It was only recently that Rachel had begun to drink coffee. They sat there for a while just sipping the coffee, then Rachel said, "I have to call Adam and Joe. I have to find out what they are doing to catch Salim. He was going to murder Karen, Heather, and Johnny. He's a monster."

Aunt Ruthie said, "We have to make a lot of changes. We have six people now in this house, and we also have to decide what to do about your dad. I think it is safe now to bring him here so we can look after him."

Just then, Aunt Ruthie's phone pinged. It was Adam. "I have amazing news! Leo is back. This morning he opened his eyes. It is like a miracle. He seems to be all there."

Aunt Ruthie gasped loudly. Rachel just looked at her with a quizzical look. "Your dad is awake," Aunt Ruthie said.

"I knew it, I knew it! He was there when I talked to him, and I knew he's coming back to us."

Aunt Ruthie said to Adam who was still on the phone, "So what now? Can we bring him to New York? There should be no more danger with Salim gone."

Adam said, "We just have to get the doctors to check him out, after all he has been in a coma for a year. I don't think he will just jump out of bed. We will check him out and then I will call you and give you an update."

Aunt Ruthie hung up the phone and hugged Rachel. "Now we have to make room for seven of us." They both had tears in their eyes. Slowly, one by one, Johnny, Karen, and Heather moseyed on into the kitchen, wiping cobwebs from their eyes. They were obviously a little bewildered at their surroundings as they settled in around the kitchen table.

Johnny again wanted to know where his mommy and daddy were. Rachel told him the good news, "We will see daddy soon, but mommy is in heaven. We can talk to mommy and I believe she can hear us, but she cannot talk to us."

Uncle Joe came into the kitchen. It got crowded around the table, and Aunt Ruthie got busy making dinner. Rachel was thinking about bringing dad to them and finding Salim.

CHAPTER 21

AMMAN, JORDAN

In New York, General Yousef Malik was extremely upset. He just got a call that five of the employees in the Embassy, including Salim and four of his people, had been involved in very serious crimes. He had been involved with Salim for years and had helped him get the relationship with the Jordanian government. He had risen in the Diplomatic Corps, from the Military Attaché in Tel Aviv to running security in New York. He helped Salim establish a lab in New York when he said he needed some materials that he could only get in the States. He transferred Salim and his assistants to the New York Embassy and gave him a free hand.

When Yaya and Ishy disappeared, he found out from contacts he had in the United States Government that they were being held as terrorists. He made several attempts to get them released without success. Now he was confronted with murder, kidnapping, attempted arson, and Salim skipping with an Embassy plane. His attempts to reach the plane had been unsuccessful. Salim was creating an international scandal that his country could not afford, given how reliant his government was on the U.S. General Malik was very conflicted. if he outed Salim, he was putting his career, and possibly his life, in danger. He needed to talk to Salim to get the full story and then decide on his next action.

Salim's plane was heading for Amman, Jordan. While sitting back, he was reviewing the past year. It had been a disaster. He wanted to kidnap and keep Leo and his children. He wanted Leo, so he could get out of him what he knew about the genetic soup and its effects on him. He suspected that he knew a lot more than he let on. Having his kids would be both beneficial and a bargaining tool to get him to cooperate and to find out if they were affected by the "soup." The plan fell apart when Leo woke up as he shot April. She was just extra baggage, and he owed him blood for blood. Leo's father had killed Adina and now he killed Leo's wife. His son would be later. Salim wanted to subdue Leo with the ether, but Leo must have heard the shot in spite of the silencer. He jumped up and Salim instinctively, without thinking, shot him in the head. Leo tumbled out of the bed and lay there dead. He checked his pulse, he was dead. How could he be alive? He could not understand. He should have used the ether on him first, then shot April. Just one debacle after another. The research on the children yielded no results; and now Saud and Raja were dead, and Yaya and Ishy were in the hands of some American service and he was on the run. He had no idea what the reception would be in Amman. He saw that General Malik was trying to reach him. His phone showed one missed call after another. He did not know what to say to him. It was better to ignore the calls for now.

While he was in the air, he called the Crown Plaza Hotel in Eilat. Eilat was the southernmost city in Israel and had a small port and the best snorkeling in the Middle East. Aqaba, in Jordan, was next to Eilat. They were literally connected to each other. If these were not countries with strict borders, you could take a walk down the beach and start in Israel and continue in Jordan without breaking stride. Salim booked a suite in the Israeli hotel beginning today without an ending date. He used the name Suliman Sarmuk, a name he had used before when he wanted to go under the radar. He had a forged Israeli passport, citizenship papers and credit cards with that name, and an address in Gedera. Gedera was a town he played in when he was young and where he owned a house under that name. Ironically, it was where he met Leo when they were children before the 1948 war. The house he now owned belonged to Leo's uncle then. He chuckled to himself. He had to have a way out if it got dangerous, and Suliman cannot or will not help him out.

When he landed in Amman, the plane went to the VIP section and Salim went through security and Customs. Using his diplomatic credentials, he did so fast and without a problem. He took a taxi to the Sheraton Amman Al Nabil Hotel and checked into a suite. Salim figured that his good times with the Jordanian money train would soon be over. He thought that he might as well enjoy the benefits as long as he could. He was still not sure what was awaiting him. He knew he had to plot a way out of Jordan. He did not know if Israel was safer; but he figured that if Jordan wanted him gone, he would disappear forever, probably in a deep hole. In Israel, at least, he would face a court system.

As soon as Salim got to his room, he took a hot shower, put on one of those fluffy bath robes, and settled into a chair. He looked at his phone and saw he had now several missed calls from the General, as well as a couple of messages from him. He listened to the messages, they were short. "Call me as soon as you can." "Where are you? Call me right away."

Salim sighed and dialed the General. "Where are you and what is going on?" General Malik barked as soon as Salim said hello. Salim held the phone away from his ear as the General yelled a few more choice and colorful words into the phone.

Salim said calmly, "I am in Amman, at the Sheraton Amman Al Nabil hotel. Is this a secure phone?" he asked. After General Malik assured him that the call was secure, he continued, "I had to get out of the States quickly after Raja went rogue."

The General clucked loudly and said, "Saud is dead and Yaya and Ishy are in the custody of the New York police for murder and kidnapping. The FBI and the New York and Cincinnati police departments are looking for you and Raja for murder, kidnapping, attempted murder, and attempted murder by arson." The General took a breath and asked, "Is Raja with you?"

Salim, after hearing the list of charges, tried to keep himself calm. He said, "Raja had an accident on the way here. He fell out of the plane."

General Malik, with surprise in his voice said, "Did you say Raja fell out of the plane? How did that happen?"

"Yes, I said Raja fell out of the plane. He tripped near the open door, maybe he jumped. Anyway, he had to go." Salim went on to give the story he rehearsed. "Raja did all the killing and the kidnapping. At the end, he killed Saud and tried to frame him. He set up gasoline cans at the lab where he kept the children, and he was going to kill them. He had the timers all set up. I was lucky I got there when I did. I was on my way to JFK to fly to my lab in Israel. I wanted to pick up a few things from the lab in the Bronx. It's when I walked in and surprised Raja. I was just in time to stop him from burning the place down with the children alive in it. Saud was already dead with a bullet and a can of gas next to his body. Raja said Saud committed suicide; but before he shot himself, he locked the children up, and set up the gasoline cans with timers to kill them and burn down the building." He continued, "Of course, I did not believe any of it but did not let Raja know my doubts. I could hear police cars and sirens blazing, converging on the building. I knew we had to get out, and we narrowly missed the incoming police. I was able to convince Raja to leave with me.

As I am sure you can understand, I had to change my plans quickly and arrange for the Embassy plane to take us to Jordan. You can check my story. I had booked a flight with El Al; but after what I saw at the lab in the Bronx, I figured it was best that I get him out of the country. I called the hangar, got to the plane, and we took off. On the way, we were throwing some stuff out of the plane and Raja clumsily fell out."

General Malik chuckled, "He had a terrible accident. I guess he deserved it. Listen Salim, you stay at the hotel. I will see you when I get there. I will fly out as soon as I can. We have to clean this up."

Salim knew when he hung up the phone that the General did not buy any of it. He thought to himself, cleaning it up means doing away with me! I have to get out of Jordan. A plan formed in his mind as he went downstairs and asked the desk clerk to arrange for a rental car. The clerk dialed the rental desk and told Salim a car will be brought to the hotel entrance. As soon as Salim took care of the paperwork with the car rental agent, he got into the car and left immediately for Aqaba, a 200-mile trip. While on the road, he called the Al Manara Hotel, a luxury Marriott hotel, and booked a room, this time with his own credit card. When he arrived in Akaba, he checked into the hotel and then booked a class with a diving school for the next morning. He made sure that they would have the gear for him. He was planning his demise on the fly. He ordered room service and wrote a note to General Malik.

Dear General Malik,

You have been a great mentor and helped me with my work and my mission to advance humanity. I have let you down with my lack of success and my bad choice in people that I engaged and used in my work. I know you will have a lot of explaining to do, but I have to remove an embarrassment and so I must martyr myself. I will go into the sea and meet Allah and ask forgiveness and hope to be redeemed. Thank you and goodbye.

Your servant and friend,
Salim Malek

He read the note over and thought, short and sweet. He placed the keys to the rental car, some of his money, and the personal and diplomatic ID papers on the night table. Then he took the forged papers, some of the money, and his phone and placed them all in a sealed plastic bag. He went to the bathroom and burned his real Israeli ID papers and flushed the remnants down the toilet. He smiled as he said goodbye to Salim.

In the morning Salim purchased a wetsuit and fins and a mask at the hotel store. He went back to his room, taped the plastic bag with his money and papers to his back, put on his wetsuit and stuffed the flippers in the front of his wetsuit hoping he would look a little overweight. He placed the mask under his chin hoping it would not be noticed when he was given another. He checked the room thoroughly one more time and placed a Do Not Disturb sign on the outside of his door as he left. He then went to look for the Akaba deep diving school. He went to the shore where several people were gathered near a shack, all putting on diving gear. Salim was fitted with a tank, weights, fins, a mask, and a flashlight. Before they went out to the reefs, they went into the shallow water to be instructed and to practice. Salim, soon to be Suliman, fastened the weights, which wore like a belt, to his waist. When the group finally left for the reef, he trailed behind. When he felt no one was near him or paying attention, he dropped the tank and the weights as well as the extra mask and the extra flippers. He took the flippers out of his suit, put on the flippers and the extra mask he brought, and set off for the Eilat shore. He prayed that the instructor will be too preoccupied with the others in the group. Goodbye Salim, he thought again to himself, and hello Suliman.

CHAPTER 22

LOOKING FOR SALIM

General Malik arrived in Amman in the morning and called the Sheraton Amman Al Nabil hotel, only to find out Salim had checked out. He was furious. In short order, he discovered from the desk clerk that Salim rented a car and left. The General knew that the whole adventure with Salim was on him. He was the one who recommended that Jordan work with him. He helped procure millions of dollars and had allowed Salim to operate illegally in the United States under his protection. Now Salim just ran off and left him holding the bag. He called a friend of his in the General Intelligence Directorate, the equivalent to the CIA and Mossad in Jordan. He asked his friend to help him locate Salim. As it turned out, the rental car company had trackers on all their cars. In a very short period of time, his friend called him and told him that they were able to determine that the car was now in Akaba. He further told him that he made some inquiries in Akaba, a relatively small area with a finite number of hotels; and

Salim was staying in the Marriott Al Manara Hotel. The General ordered his car and sped to a military airport nearby, commandeered a helicopter and two soldiers that were guarding it, and ordered it flown to Akaba. Once there they landed at another military facility and with the two soldiers in tow, they obtained a staff car and drove to the hotel.

The General walked straight up to the desk and demanded to see the manager. When the manager came out and saw the General with the soldiers, he quickly surrendered the information that indeed a Salim Malek was registered and offered to take them to his room. Once at the door, the General ripped off the Do Not Disturb sign and ordered the manager to open the door. With his service revolver out in his hand and the two soldiers with their weapons at the ready as well, they stormed into the suite. Salim was not there, of course. They searched the whole place and found all the Jordanian papers he left behind and the note. The General read the note several times and finally turned to the manager who was still lurking in the hallway. "Where is Salim Malek?" he barked.

The poor manager, obviously nervous, said "I understand he booked a scuba class for this morning; the instructor came back a while ago and said that he was missing."

The General raised his voice even more, "What do you mean he is missing? Is he lost?"

The manager said, "He somehow disappeared in the water. They found his gear, but he was gone. There are strong currents in that area. We tell everyone to be very careful. I think without the flippers and the weights, he probably drowned."

"You are saying that in your experience, without fins and a mask, it's unlikely he survived?"

"Many people drown here."

The General said to no one in particular, "That is a coward's way to die, not a martyr's." He gathered all of Salim's things, handed them to the nearest soldier, and motioned them all out of the room. He turned to the manager and said, "Not a word about this to anyone, you understand?" The poor man just nodded his head. The General left for his trip back to Amman and the storm that awaited him from his superiors.

Salim, now Suliman, stepped out of the water with his wetsuit, goggles, and fins. He looked like just another of the dozens of tourists in the water and on the beach. As he walked to the Crown Plaza, he fished his documents out from his back, walked into the hotel, stepped up to the check-in counter, and asked for his room key. The clerk asked for his name. He told him "Suliman Sarmuk." The clerk noted that he checked in online, examined his driver's license and made a copy, took an imprint of his credit card, and then returned them to him and gave him the key to his suite. Step one, Salim thought. Now he had to disappear so that the border police, the national police, or the Mossad would not find him. He hoped that General Malik, would buy the suicide. He knew that the FBI, New York police, the Cincinnati police, and whoever had Yaya and Ishy, were communicating with the Jordanians. He hoped that they would believe the suicide, too. He had to get clothing and personal items before he left. He was anxious to get away from Eilat and get to his new life at his home in Gedera.

Back in Cincinnati, Joe and Adam were at the CIA hospital talking to Leo. They gently gave him the bad news that his wife April had died from her wounds at the same time that he was shot and that his children were kidnapped but were rescued last night. They told him he was in a coma for a year and that it seemed his bullet injury had healed, and the tests and EKG remarkably showed no permanent damage. All three found the coincident eerie, that he came out of the coma almost simultaneously with his children being rescued.

Leo was anxious to see them, and Adam promised that he would make the arrangements to take him to his sister's house as soon as the doctors cleared him. They asked him if he felt strong enough to be debriefed by them and he indicated that he was.

Over the next several hours he told them about Salim, his childhood friend, the work they did together with Professor Gill, and the accident that took his wife and son, as well as his parents and sister. He told them, "I must have heard the shot that killed April because I remember waking up, jumping up in bed, seeing Salim, and then the lights went out. A while ago I started hearing a lot of what was going on around me. Once a nurse must have brought a boyfriend in, and I heard them talking and kissing. Then I heard Rachel. Wait," he stopped and looked at them. "I thought you said that the children were kidnapped?"

Joe told him, "Rachel hid that night and was not taken. She has been with your sister all this time. Rachel actually helped us find where Salim took them. He found out that you are alive. We guess he did not know that you are in a coma, and so he decided to kill the children and his man who was watching them."

Leo, obviously getting emotional, said, "But why was Salim in the States and what did he want with my children? Why did he kill April?"

Adam said, "There is a lot we don't know, but we will find out." Leo wanted to know if they had Salim. Joe told him that he and one of his men got away. Leo's jaws clenched as well as his fists, "He has to pay, we have to find him!" Adam assured him that they were working on it and would find him.

The CIA in general and Adam and Joe in particular had good relations with most security organizations in the Middle East. They contacted both the Mossad and the General Intelligence Directorate. The Mossad knew of Salim and his work for the Jordanians. They also knew about the lab. They reported that the lab had very recently been closed and Salim's whereabouts were unknown. The Directorate had more interesting information. They reported that Salim arrived in Amman without his sidekick, who the pilots reported "fell" out of the plane. Their contact in the directorate told them that Salim wound up in Akaba where he drowned in an apparent suicide.

The following day Joe and Adam went to see Leo again. They relayed to him all that they had learned and told him that the consensus of the two agencies was that Salim was dead. Leo listened and said nothing. He thought that there was absolutely no way that the Salim he knew would kill himself. He was sure that Salim was alive, on the run, and hiding probably with an assumed identity.

Several days later the CIA doctors released Leo. As he was wheeled out, all of the health professionals who looked after him for over a year were cheering and clapping, and he gave them hugs and high fives, thanking them with tears in his eyes.

Leo's reunion with his children was very emotional. They all cried and hugged and cried some more. He did not stop thanking Ruth and Joe, telling them that he could never repay them. After some time talking to his children and Ruth and Joe, he decided that he wanted to move back to Israel. Staying in the country where his beloved April was killed and his children endured the trauma of a year in the hands of sick people, did not seem plausible to him. He did not want to relive the horrible tragedy or have his children feel insecure; and when he spoke to the children and Ruth and Joe, they all agreed. What he did not reveal was that he wanted to find Salim. He wanted revenge. He wanted him dead. Leo figured that while he went to Israel to look into relocating, he would leave the children with Ruth and use the time to find Salim.

Ruth and Joe had no problem taking care of the children, but they did not want Leo to go alone. That was fine with Rachel who immediately volunteered to go with him. Leo resisted the idea, but in the end, he relented. And so, a couple of months after waking up from a coma, Leo and Rachel were on their way to Israel to plan for another life-changing move.

Suliman, formerly Salim, stayed a couple of more days in Eilat. He then took a flight to Tel Aviv and from there rented a car and drove to the Dan Hotel on the Tel Aviv shore. He knew that he could not go to his lab or his apartment; he needed to get to the hideaway he prepared years ago. It was a house in Gedera that belonged to a Jewish family. As a matter of fact, it was Leo's uncle who owned it and he bought it from his estate. Some years ago, he transferred the deed to Suliman Sarmuk. He figured that he was not only safer there, but he was also close to the border and knew every inch of the area. His village was no longer there, his parents had passed away, and he had lost contact with his family on the other side of the border a long time ago. It was ideal for hiding in plain sight. After a few days he returned the rental car and purchased a used motor bike. The trip to Gedera was uneventful, and he knew he would have a lot of work to do to bring the old house up to date. He looked forward to the physical labor it would require. He thought it would take his mind off the disastrous year that just transpired and some terrible decisions he had made. Luckily, he diverted some of the millions that he got from the Jordanians, so money was not a problem for him. it was stashed in the house, as were some of the weapons he acquired over the years.

When Leo arrived in Israel with Rachel at his side, he was overcome with grief. He missed his wife April and was upset about what his children had gone through. They checked into a small hotel on a street by the sea, not far from the American Embassy. Not long after their arrival, they were met by a young man who introduced himself as Shalom Or. Leo thought it was a beautiful name. In Hebrew, shalom means peace, and or means light. Shalom told them that he was with the Mossad and that he had been asked by the local CIA office to help Leo in his search for Salim and also provide security. He also had a car at his disposal. Leo assumed that Joe and Adam arranged it, and he was grateful.

The first place they decided to go was to Israel's Mossad bureau in Jerusalem. Israel monitored all aircraft in their neighboring countries. Shalom escorted them into a building that looked like an ordinary apartment building in an ordinary neighborhood. They would have never guessed that the most famous spy agency in the world had offices here. They went to a room buzzing with different machines, and a young woman greeted them and told them she would assist them. Leo told her that he was looking for information on a private plane that would have flown into Jordan around the date of the rescue. After sitting down at a computer terminal and pressing a bunch of keys, she came up with a list of planes. Some were commercial and some were private. Leo asked, "Would you know if it was an Embassy plane? It would have come from the United States."

She pressed some keys again and said, "There was one plane that we believe was a small Jordanian government plane that landed in Amman. The next day we have another government plane coming in from the United States, as well, also landing in Amman. We have no other information on the first plane, but we know the second plane passenger was General Yousef Malik, the Military Attaché to the Jordanian Embassy in the United States. He flew in from New York.

When Shalom heard that he said, "We have good relations with the Jordanian General Intelligence Directorate. I will contact them and see what I can find out." Shalom escorted them into a conference room and left them for a while. Rachel took it all in. She loved all the cloak and dagger stuff.

She asked her dad, "Were you a spy in the CIA?"

Leo chuckled and said, "No, I was an analyst. I mainly looked at documents and data and helped the different departments understand their meaning and intent. I never worked in the field or did any spying." Rachel looked disappointed. She had hoped for a much more intense involvement.

Shalom came back and told them that he spoke to a contact in the Directorate, and that he would get back to him in a few hours. He suggested that since it was noon that they get lunch and maybe walk around a bit.

They went to a restaurant that had tables outside and ordered plates of traditional middle eastern food: falafel, which are deep fried balls of ground chickpeas, with pita, a kind of flatbread, salad cut up really small, and sauces called tahini and hummus. After lunch, they walked around town. Rachel wanted to see the Western Wall of the ancient Jewish Temple, but Shalom thought they should get back and see what had come in from the Directorate. They returned to the Mossad offices and were ushered into the conference room again. Shalom left them there and when he returned a few minutes later, he had a sheet of paper with him. He said, "This is very interesting and very conclusive. Salim was on that first plane. Raja was not. He evidently fell out of the plane somewhere over the ocean, at least that is what Salim said. After he landed, he evidently drove to Akaba, went deep sea diving, and drowned. I was told that he left a suicide note. So, it seems that the story has a happy ending, or at least an ending."

Leo and Rachel both looked at him questionably. Leo

spoke up first, "I heard that Salim committed suicide. Did they say how he did it? What happened exactly?"

Shalom looked confused and asked, "What do you mean?"

"Did they find the body?"

Shalom said, "I know they were looking for it, but they did not find him. I understand it is very rare to find a drowning victim in these waters. The currents are very strong and the water very deep. They have a lot of drownings. They did find the tank, the fins, and his mask."

Rachel chimed in now, "Let me summarize, Salim gets rid of Saud and Raja, abandons Yaya and Ishy, returns to Jordan, and then decides to kill himself. Leaves a suicide note and then joins a class for scuba diving, gets into the water, takes off his gear, and disappears in the deep blue waters. Did I get that right?"

Leo looked at her approvingly and then turned to Shalom, "Sounds so nice and neat, doesn't it?

Shalom looked thoughtful, "I guess it is too neat. So what do you want to do next?"

Leo replied, "Next we look at any and all men that seemed to appear suddenly in Eilat. My guess is he had an alias at the ready and came in with that identity." Shalom suggested he take them back to the hotel and arrange for a flight to Eilat for the next day. Rachel asked if they could visit the Western Wall before they left. Shalom made the arrangements.

The Western Wall, or the Kotel as the Israelis called it, looked huge to Rachel. She had seen it in pictures, but they did not do it justice. The wall was from the Sacred Jewish Temple and dated back thousands of years. There was a special section for women. Orthodox Jews practice separa-tion of men and women when they pray. The responsibility for the wall was placed in the hands of the orthodox Rabbinate, and they enforced religious laws strictly. Shalom remained behind watching Rachel, while Leo went to the men's side. They thanked Shalom for his patience, and he drove them back to their hotel in Tel Aviv. Their hotel was literally facing the beach. Rachel went downstairs after dinner and sat there watching the sunset and the waves reflecting the last rays.

The next day, Shalom picked them up and drove a short distance to the Tel Aviv airport and a flight to Eilat. Rachel, who always heard what a small country Israel is, was awed by the Negev desert. It was vast and went on and on as they flew over it. It was also mountainous. She always assumed that desert was sand, so to see mountains in the desert was a new reality for her.

They arrived in Eilat and when they stepped out of the plane, she was shocked at the heat that met her. It was not only hot; it was hot wind. They took a cab to hotel row. Shalom asked Leo, "How do you want to start?"

Leo said "Let's start by going to the hotels nearest the beach and see if they remember a guest in a bathing suit or more likely a wetsuit, which I imagine he wore, because he would have had his identification papers and money with him. Perhaps if it was the first time they saw him coming in, maybe he made an impression. They decided to start from opposite sides of the beach. Leo and Rachel would start on the left and Shalom would begin from the right. After a few hours they met in one of the cafes by the beach, almost exactly in the middle, and compared notes. They had several names from the hotels, and they now had to work to narrow it down. They also had the nationalities and addresses of these men. They exchanged the lists, Shalom taking Leo's list and Leo taking Shalom's. As was expected, they had no Jordanians and no Salim. There was a name that raised a long memory in Leo. One of the names was an Israeli Arab who lived in Gedera. Leo remembered that was where he met Salim. They decided to go back to the Crown Plaza and question the clerk some more.

Once they got to the hotel, they asked the clerk to show them the check-in information for Suliman Sarmuk. The clerk called the manager out, and Shalom showed him his credentials. They were ushered into an office, and the manager brought them the information they requested. The room was booked the day before by phone and was not occupied until the following day. The guest stayed a few days and left. The hotel had a copy of the guest's driver's license and credit card record. They requested and received copies of both. They were not very good copies. Leo thought he recognized Salim but was not 100% sure. It was a really fuzzy picture. Then Rachel looked at the driver's license and pointed to the picture. Her father looked at her quizzically. Rachel said, "The scar, look at the scar." Leo looked at the copy of the license. He could see a scar on the throat of the individual. It was Salim, no doubt. While they took a cab back to the airport, Shalom called his office and gave them the information to follow up. By the time they arrived at the Tel Aviv airport, Shalom had the rundown on Suliman Sarmuk. He materialized five years ago out of thin air. There was no entry or exit record, into or out of Israel. The address he gave in Gedera was purchased by Suliman five years ago from the estate of Saul Meir. Leo said excitedly, "It has to be him. That house belonged to my aunt and uncle. They died years ago. My cousin Saul then died six or seven years ago. Our families were at odds, and we did not have anything to do with each other or with Saul for many, many years.

Leo thought that before they called the troops, they should make sure that this man, Suliman, was in fact Salim. He remembered his summer in Gedera. He had fond memories of the place. Leo was five when he was last there, and he wondered if he would recognize the Meir house. Gedera was not far from Tel Aviv and not very congested. Leo thought that perhaps it would be prudent for them to check out the house and make sure Suliman was Salim. He knew they would have to be very careful not to be detected.

Rachel thought that was a great idea. In the morning she and Leo, with Shalom at the wheel, drove to Gedera. Leo was shocked at how different the place looked; but then again, it was a very long time ago since he last saw it. When they arrived, they saw a whole section of new attached homes, a few apartment buildings, and meadows with sunflowers. Finally, they came to another area that Leo thought he recognized, though he was not sure. These were older homes, more spacious with more property, but most of them looked shabbier and more neglected. As they drove through these streets, Rachel suddenly told Shalom, "Stop!"

Shalom did so, and Leo asked her, "Why are we stopping?"

Rachel said through clenched teeth, "It's Salim!" Both Leo and Shalom looked at where she was pointing but did not see anyone that they could identify. There was a worker in a yard far ahead, but they could hardly make out what he was wearing, let alone who it was. Shalom produced binoculars, and Leo peered through them. Sure enough, it was Salim working in the yard with a cut-off shirt and a red bandana around his forehead.

Leo took out his phone and snapped a whole slew of pictures, then turned to Shalom and asked, "Do you have a weapon?"

"I do, why are you asking?"

"I am going to take Salim down."

Shalom said, "That is not a good idea. I am sure the office will want to handle it. Let's just watch him, and I will call it in." Leo was not happy. He was looking forward to confronting Salim, but he relented. He did not want to give into his rage. He wanted to be a good role model for Rachel, who he knew was looking forward to avenging her mom. He did not want to be on the wrong side of the Mossad or the Israeli Police. Shalom reported their sighting of Salim, who they now knew was going by Suliman Sarmuk. Shalom explained to his boss that with the help of Jordan's General Intelligence Directorate and some good footwork, they traced Salim.

They stayed at the same spot as a contingent of agents from the Mossad surrounded the house on Freedom Road. It was a brief fight. Salim ran into the house when he saw the agents approaching; but he did not see, or anticipate, that agents were waiting in the back of his house, knowing it was his only way out. He ran right into their arms. As they were taking Salim out of the house in handcuffs, Shalom, Leo and Rachel approached. Salim looked up in surprise as Leo came near him and uttered just one word, "YOU!"

Leo, with all his bottled-up anger said nothing. He just

hauled off and punched Salim in his gut as hard as he could. As Salim bent over in pain, Leo said with clenched teeth, "This is for April."

Just then, Rachel approached and before anyone could stop her or intervene, she kicked him as hard as she could in his groin. Salim yelped and doubled over in even more pain. Rachel said, "That is for my brother and sisters." Leo and Rachel walked away with Shalom trailing. Salim just looked after them, wondering how they found him as he thought his plan was perfect. The Mossad agents, who looked amused with Leo and Rachel, said nothing. They just straightened Salim up and loaded him into a van. Rachel thought it was ironic that Salim was found and caught on a street named Freedom Road.

EPILOGUE

Leo wanted Salim dead, and he wanted to be the executioner. Letting Shalom talk him out of killing Salim was the best thing that had happened, for him and for Rachel. As it turned out, there were worse fates than death. Shalom told him later that the Mossad, after they got all they needed from Salim, turned him over to Jordan's General Intelligence Directorate. He was sure that his fate in Jordan would be harsher than any sentence he would receive in the United States or in Israel. The Directorate promised that Salim would not be a problem for either country again. The Israeli government confiscated Salim's house, and Leo bought the former Meir home for what was a very low price. You could say it was the Israeli government's way of thanking the family for exposing Salim and the Jordanian connection and making up for their loss.

Heather, Karen, and Johnny followed Leo and Rachel and arrived in Israel joining Leo and Rachel. Rachel was only sad that she would be so far from Aunt Ruthie and Uncle Joe. They did come a few months later to Israel to throw a big Bat Mitzvah party for Rachel as they promised they would. Rachel did not forget her promise that they could have the party as soon as she was reunited with her brother and sisters. She chanted all the parts which she remembered perfectly to the delight of the whole family and their new community.

It took the children a while to recover from their ordeal and adjust to their new country. In Cincinnati before the attack, Leo and April spoke to the children in Hebrew at home, so their adjustment in the schools was quick. Leo accepted a position with the university's Languages Department and also decided to accept a moonlighting job with the Mossad.

Their new house was close to the border of what was called Judea and Samaria. The area was taken over by Israel in the 1967 Six-Day War. Unlike other areas of the border, there was no wall, just a fence. It allowed villagers to pass through and many Israelis to venture across, also. On a hill not far from the border, the site of a former Arab village, lived an extended family of Bedouins. The Bedouin culture went back 4,500 years. Owing to the unchangeability of desert conditions, this culture remained largely unchanged and was recognizable in the Bible. Many believe that Abraham, the father of all the Jews and Muslims, was a Bedouin. The stories of Abraham and Lot hosting angels illustrated one of the most renowned and cherished social values in Bedouin society, namely the practice of hospitality. One side of a Bedouin tent is always wide open to signify that all guests were welcome. Rachel loved to take a walk up the hill and visit their camp. She loved the smells of coffee and pita. And they always had animals running around. Camels, sheep, goats, and of course, dogs. She met a girl named Mahra who was around her age. Once a week they would meet and talk. Rachel would bring some of the salad that her dad loved to make. He would cut up peppers, cucumbers, and tomatoes really small and mix in some onions and radishes. Mahra would bring pita and goat cheese, and they would sit and eat and talk.

Rachel loved to talk to her dad as well, especially about his days with the CIA. On one occasion when Leo and Rachel were reminiscing, Rachel asked her dad about the genetic experiments and how he felt about her abilities. She wanted to know if he thought it was worthwhile to continue that research, after all, it worked with her. Leo became very thoughtful and said, "I think that what I did was foolish and thoughtless. While it has affected you, and so far, not adversely, we really don't know what else it has done or will do to you. We also don't know if it has or will affect your brother and sisters, or for that matter, me. I think that the animal world needs the abilities that nature has endowed them with; but they each are unique, and so are we. The animals have given us many gifts, and continue giving. We need to use the God-given talents we have and enjoy the abilities that the animals have. So many creatures help us in our daily life. So the answer is 'no.' I do not think we should continue with the experiments. You see, animals are our gift. We have our own special abilities, and we should be satisfied with them."

Rachel continued to amaze her teachers. She was admitted into the Academy for Gifted Children on her way to an accelerated college program and looked forward to joining the Mossad or the CIA when she graduated, whichever service would take her. She knew that her talents would be valuable, and she was determined to use them for good. Both agencies probably would fight for her services.

THE END

ABOUT THE AUTHOR

Rony is an Israeli-born Ameri-can. He grew up in Tel Aviv, across the street from the beach.

He arrived in New York with his family as a teen, obtaining an Associate degree from New York City Community College after graduating from High School, later receiving an Accounting degree from Queens College after four years of night school. Rony served in the US Army during the Vietnam War, and earned a Master's in Business Administration from LIU. Licensed as a CPA, Rony concentrated in tax and financial Consulting.

Rony always loved to write poetry and essays. It led him to initiate, write and edit a client newsletter for over twenty years. Some forty years ago Rony joined Rotary International, a service and charity organization, where he also started, wrote and edited a newsletter until 2019. Rony is still very active with Rotary, raising money for many causes and organizations.

Rony and his wife Ana live on Long Island in New York,

they have six children and twelve grandchildren and love to spend time with them.

Rachel was born in Rony's mind, while waiting for a friend in a restaurant, some 20 years ago. He still has the napkin on which he wrote the opening chapter. When asked why it took this long to finish the book, he laughed and said he waited for his grandchildren to get old enough to help him edit the book, which indeed they did.